2 4 APR 2018

KT-549-594

WITHDRAWN FROM
BROMLEY LIBRARIES

Renewals

0333 370 4700

arena.yourlondonlibrary.net/
web/bromley

THE LONDON BOROUGH
www.bromley.gov.uk

Please return/renew this item
by the last date shown.
Books may also be renewed by
phone and Internet.

Bromley Libraries

30128 80326 428 5

Books by Tom Palmer

The Foul Play series (in reading order)
FOUL PLAY
DEAD BALL
OFF SIDE
KILLER PASS

For younger readers

THE SECRET FOOTBALL CLUB

The Football Academy series (in reading order)
BOYS UNITED
STRIKING OUT
THE REAL THING
READING THE GAME
FREE KICK
CAPTAIN FANTASTIC

KILLER PASS

TOM PALMER

PUFFIN

PUFFIN BOOKS

Published by the Penguin Group
Penguin Books Ltd, 80 Strand, London WC2R 0RL, England
Penguin Group (USA) Inc., 375 Hudson Street, New York, New York 10014, USA
Penguin Group (Canada), 90 Eglinton Avenue East, Suite 700, Toronto, Ontario, Canada M4P 2Y3
(a division of Pearson Penguin Canada Inc.)
Penguin Ireland, 25 St Stephen's Green, Dublin 2, Ireland (a division of Penguin Books Ltd)
Penguin Group (Australia), 250 Camberwell Road, Camberwell, Victoria 3124, Australia
(a division of Pearson Australia Group Pty Ltd)
Penguin Books India Pvt Ltd, 11 Community Centre, Panchsheel Park, New Delhi – 110 017, India
Penguin Group (NZ), 67 Apollo Drive, Rosedale, North Shore 0632, New Zealand
(a division of Pearson New Zealand Ltd)
Penguin Books (South Africa) (Pty) Ltd, 24 Sturdee Avenue, Rosebank,
Johannesburg 2196, South Africa

Penguin Books Ltd, Registered Offices: 80 Strand, London WC2R 0RL, England

puffinbooks.com

First published 2010
007

Text copyright © Tom Palmer, 2010
All rights reserved

The moral right of the author has been asserted

Set in Sabon MT Std 12.5/17.25 pt
Typeset by Palimpsest Book Production Ltd, Falkirk, Stirlingshire
Printed in Great Britain by Clays Ltd, St Ives plc

Except in the United States of America, this book is sold subject to the condition that it shall not, by
way of trade or otherwise, be lent, re-sold, hired out, or otherwise circulated without the publisher's
prior consent in any form of binding or cover other than that in which it is published and without a
similar condition including this condition being imposed on the subsequent purchaser

British Library Cataloguing in Publication Data
A CIP catalogue record for this book is available from the British Library

ISBN: 978-0-141-33118-8

www.greenpenguin.co.uk

MIX
Paper from
responsible sources
FSC
www.fsc.org   FSC® C018179

Penguin Books is committed to a sustainable
future for our business, our readers and our planet.
This book is made from Forest Stewardship
Council™ certified paper.

This book is for Diane Baker and all the children and teachers at Ghyllgrove Junior School, Basildon

CONTENTS

Friday

Saturday

WEDNESDAY

SURVEILLANCE

Danny Harte saw more than he had expected to over the fence. He was looking into the large garden of a *very* large house. The house backed on to a thick area of woodland, where Danny was carrying out a vital piece of surveillance.

There were five windows on the ground floor. All with lights on. Four of the windows had curtains or blinds drawn. But through the fifth window Danny could see a massive TV screen. So big it had to be a cinema screen, not a TV screen at all. He'd never seen one like that in the shops. It was amazing.

But he could see more than that.

A gold-plated mirror on the wall next to the screen.

Several huge vases full of fancy flowers.

A giant model of a Ferrari 300 parked between

3

two L-shaped sofas that looked like it was being used as a coffee table.

But none of these things surprised Danny as much as the fence that stood between him and these millionaires' houses. For a start it was at least four metres high, with the top metre angling out towards the wood. It was tangled with razor wire. And, every few paces, it displayed a sign, black on yellow, showing a man being electrocuted.

Danny wondered just how anyone would get over this fence.

Feeling uncomfortable, he switched his crouching position from one leg to another. He could feel pins and needles coming on. And that was the last thing he needed. He was on private land. He may need to run away.

But fleeing from the investigation was the last thing Danny wanted. His main concern was how a burglar might get into the houses he was watching. He thought back to the book he'd been reading, a book about house-breaking. Burglars explaining how to get in and out without being caught. Danny was reading the book to help him with his latest investigation. An investigation of a crime that he wanted to solve more than any of the others he'd solved before.

An investigation into a string of burglaries at City FC players' houses. His team – the team he had supported passionately all his life. And the latest crime had been on this street just days ago.

The street was actually a gated community of ten houses, and among the rich people living there were three footballers, one pop star and a supermodel.

So, what would a burglar do now? He had to think the way they thought. That was how to solve a crime.

Was this the way they'd come in?

The only other option was the front of the house.

But that meant going through the main entrance on to the street. And past two security guards. That option also meant avoiding being seen by at least seven security cameras Danny had spotted up and down the street. It was a bad option. So how was it that a burglar had got into this gated community and into the house of footballer John Hawley?

Danny was baffled. It had to be impossible. But it had happened. Anyway, it was going to be almost impossible to solve this crime.

If Danny *was* going to solve it, it would be by

thinking like a burglar. That was why he'd been reading about how to burgle. That was why he was here watching footballers' houses from a wood.

Danny's focus on the task wavered for just a second as he thought about the football team that had brought him here.

His team, City FC, were playing a first-leg away tie in the knockout stages of Champions League right now. At Real Madrid.

Danny checked around to see that there really was no one nearby. Knowing he was taking a risk – albeit a really quick one, he promised himself – he switched on his mini-radio, slipping in his earpiece.

At first Danny thought he had the wrong channel. All he could hear was noise. He went to retune the set, but then heard the voice of the commentator trying to break through the chaos.

'. . . City FC drawing one–one here at the Bernabéu . . . but after a killer pass the length of the pitch from Real's midfield maestro . . . and that late tackle . . . penalty to Real . . . chance for the home team to take the lead . . .'

Danny's heart sank. He checked his watch. There were five minutes left. If Real scored now

City would lose. Probably. And getting through to the semi-finals would be a lot harder.

Danny waited for the noise on the radio to die down. Noise that was so clear Danny imagined he was there. And now he could hear the silence of the Real fans waiting for the penalty taker to step back and shoot. Then the roar of the City fans, trying to put the Real player off. The City fans would be in the top tier of the stadium, miles away from the action. But you could still hear them. Danny felt proud. He tried to picture the game in his mind, his eyes closed.

'HEY, YOU!'

Danny kept his eyes closed for a second, trying to work out who would be shouting that at the match. Then he realized that what he was hearing wasn't at the Bernabéu at all: it was in a wood overlooking a footballer's house. Right here. Right now.

That was when he felt the hand on his shoulder.

Danny ducked instinctively, hitting the ground, ready to escape. That was one more thing he'd learned from reading about burglary. Never fight. Always flee.

Hitting the ground like that worked. Danny

had opened his eyes to see a youngish man stumbling above him, his hand outstretched. But now the man – wearing a black security-guard uniform – was on his hands and knees. He'd fallen when Danny had moved away.

And because of that Danny was free to run, through the woods and along the path he'd come down. One of his two escape routes. One he'd worked out before settling down to watch. That was in the book too. A burglar had said: know your escape route like you're on a plane and might need to evacuate. And know two routes, in case one is blocked.

Danny ran fast. He could not afford to get caught – they would never believe he wasn't doing anything wrong. As he ran the smell of the woods was strong. The bark of the trees, the leaves damp and rotting in the mud.

He looked back, his lungs straining.

The security guard was close.

And then he slipped. Fatal.

Danny fell hard, his hand striking at the roots of the tree that had tripped him. He tried to scramble to his feet. But he could already feel the arms of the security guard around his legs, like a heavy rugby tackle.

For a split second, he wondered what would happen if he was caught. Could he argue that he was merely watching? Helping to solve a crime? They'd be bound to think he was the burglar, or at least involved in it somehow. Then he'd be in trouble with the police. Again. And that was a problem. This time he would end up with a police record. Or worse.

Because Danny had form. Over the last year he had been involved in helping solve several crimes. Football crimes. A combination of his two greatest loves. Football because of City FC. Solving crimes because he and his dad loved to read detective novels together.

So Danny kicked out against the security guard. Hard. Really hard.

Even though he knew it was bad to kick some-one who was just doing his job.

But he had to get away.

The grip on his legs loosened after the kick. Danny got to his feet. Then he ran. He was free.

He wanted to feel good about that, but now he was worried. What about the security guard? Was he hurt?

Danny could hear nothing behind him. So he looked back, but seeing nothing he stopped.

Still nothing.

He made his way carefully back. To check what had happened to his pursuer.

In a clearing, among the roots of a tree that was coming away from the hillside, the security guard was standing. Danny was relieved to see that.

But he was *not* relieved to see the security guard talking. Into a radio.

That meant one thing: back-up.

Danny set off running again. He'd head through the woods to the canal, not the road. The longer he stayed off the road, the longer he'd be safe. He found himself jogging at a steady pace. He was getting away. It was going to be OK.

And Danny Harte smiled: soon he would be able to find out if Real Madrid had missed that penalty. Or not.

OUT OF CHARACTER

Danny walked up Foxglove Avenue. His road. His home.

But he wasn't smiling any more.

He couldn't believe how sloppy he'd been back in the woods. Almost getting caught like that. Not good.

In the end, the Spanish champions *had* scored their penalty and won the match: 2–1. It was not a disaster. But it would be much harder to win the tie now.

But anyway, Danny knew he had to focus, he couldn't let it happen again.

That wasn't the only reason he wasn't smiling. There was another reason he was walking back home as slowly as he could.

From today, his parents were away. Getting to know each other again, they'd said. Danny knew what they really meant. He wasn't stupid. They'd been arguing a lot. This was them trying to make a go of things again.

His parents were leaving him behind for the first time. And that meant he was sharing the house with his sister. And – because he was fourteen and she was seventeen – *she* was in charge.

It was cold outside now. The temperature had dropped since Danny had been in the wood. Or maybe it had just been warmer there. There were fewer trees here. Less cover.

Danny opened the door, looking into the front room through the window as he did so. He saw his sister lounging back on the sofa, the phone to her ear, a glass of wine in the other hand.

She's making herself comfortable, he thought.

He resented that Emily could swan about the house drinking wine. She was only doing it to get at him anyway. Pretending to be an adult. Trying to remind him that he was a child.

This week was going to be a nightmare.

He shut the door quietly, pulled off his jacket and put it on a hook. If he just slung it somewhere, he knew Emily would tell him to hang it up. Being the adult – again. He didn't want to give her any opportunities to do that.

'Hey, Danny.'

Emily stood in the front room doorway. Recently something had changed about her. She'd started wearing fancy scarves around her neck. Even indoors. More evidence that she was trying to act like she was older.

'Hi,' Danny said neutrally. He was immediately suspicious. Why was she being friendly? And why, he wondered, was she grinning?

'Can I get you a drink?' Emily asked.

Danny frowned. 'I'm not allowed,' he said.

'Just a bit of wine,' she said. 'They let you when they're here.'

'No thanks,' Danny said. That was it then, Emily was obviously trying to get him into trouble.

'Tea, then?' Emily offered.

And she was still grinning. Why *was* that? Danny could hardly bear it. She was supposed to be mean to him. Not nice. But seeing as she was being nice, he'd try to be too.

'Coke?' he suggested.

'Coming up,' she said.

Danny went into the front room. Emily had two side lamps on. Not the main light. Danny flicked the main light on and leafed through the evening paper. Previews of the Real v. City game.

When Emily came back in she went to turn the main light off, then stopped herself.

Danny smiled. What *was* she up to? She always switched the main light off if he'd switched it on. It was one of the things they did to annoy each other.

But this time, nothing.

'Who were you on the phone to?' Danny asked, flicking on the teletext service. He wanted to see the other Champions League scores.

'Nobody.'

Danny looked at his sister. She was grinning again. Like she had the best secret ever and she wasn't going to tell it.

Danny decided to be direct. 'You're lying,' he said.

Emily grinned again.

Could he do nothing to annoy her?

'Come on,' he persisted, 'who was it?'

Emily sighed. 'Just a friend.'

Danny kept his eyes on her for a few seconds. But she said nothing. Then he looked away. He wasn't going to give her the satisfaction of him begging to know. So he looked back at the TV screen at the week's Champions League results:

Bayern Munich	0	AC Milan	0
Forza FC	3	Barcelona	1
Leeds United	4	Manchester United	0
Real Madrid	2	City FC	1

'Sorry, Danny,' Emily said, breaking into Danny's thoughts.

'Why?' Danny said. 'What for?'

'I'm sorry you lost.'

Danny swallowed. This was getting all too weird.

'Thanks,' he said.

'But Forza won,' Emily said cheerfully.

Forza FC was a new Italian team taking Europe by storm. They had come out of the shadow of Juventus and Inter Milan by stealing the place of another team in the Italian second division and being bankrolled by a billionaire. Like the way Milton Keynes Dons were created in the UK. At the expense of Wimbledon FC.

Danny nodded suspiciously. 'Roberts scored all three,' he said.

'I know. I watched the game.'

'You WHAT?' Danny could not believe what he was hearing.

'I watched it,' Emily confirmed, 'on the Internet.'

Danny glanced over at the computer in the corner. It was showing one of the illegal Internet sites where you could watch football for free. He was freaked out now. His sister had the evening in the house to herself and she had not spent it in the bathroom, or spent it online chatting to her friends, but had spent it watching Champions League football.

'How come?' he asked.

'I like Forza.'

'Why?'

'They're good.'

'But you hate football.'

'Hmmm,' Emily said, smiling again. 'Maybe not.' Then she stood and left the room, heading for the kitchen. She was still grinning, Danny noticed.

Danny sipped his Coke. He had to think about this clearly. In the book he'd been reading about burglars, there'd been a lot about human behaviour. Psychology. About why people start to burgle houses. And in the book there was a section about why individuals suddenly change. Be it from being good to becoming bad or, like his sister, from being mean to being nice.

With burglars it was often drugs. They got

into drugs, became addicted and started to need more money. So they robbed houses.

This meant nothing when it came to his sister. Danny was pretty sure she wouldn't be so stupid as to do drugs, even if she was an idiot. But he knew her change in behaviour meant something. If a person suddenly acted differently then something had changed in their life.

But what?

Then Danny had a crazy idea. Maybe her weirdness was more to do with Forza FC. Maybe she *was* seeing someone new. Maybe it was Sam Roberts, the footballer. She'd met him here, after all, thanks to Danny. It had been months ago. Danny had been investigating a string of robberies near the City FC stadium when he'd stumbled across Roberts' kidnapping. It was Danny's first case. And he'd solved it. As a result Roberts had come round to Danny's house to say thank you. That was how Emily had met him.

And surely the only reason she would get into football was to do with a boy. Or a man.

Then Danny shook his head. He'd been reading too many crazy crime books. That was pushing it way too far. As if his sister would be

going out with an England international footballer!

Danny shrugged and moved over to the
computer. He wanted to check his emails.

The one that he checked first was from his
friend Kofi. Kofi Danquah was the one person
Danny knew who actually worked for City FC.
And he was a player. Not a first-team player, but
he was still a player. Kofi was sixteen and had
recently come over to the UK from Ghana. He
had had a lot of trouble with his agent. Not that
Danny was a friend to the stars. This had been
another of his detective investigations, into the
corrupt agent who had brought Kofi to the UK.
With Danny's help, Kofi had managed to get the
agent arrested and secure a place at City.

Dear Danny,
Would you like to come and see me playing
for the under-eighteens? It will be my first
game for them. The game is on Saturday.
Also, if you want to meet this week in the
city centre please say so. I think you said you
are on holiday from your school this week.
With best wishes,
Kofi Danquah

Danny loved the way Kofi sent emails and texts that were so polite. He spoke like that too, always making sure he was using the right word. Danny quickly typed a message back to Kofi saying he would definitely meet him there. This was a chance to see City FC at close quarters. And to spend time with his new friend.

As he finished typing, Danny heard his sister go up the stairs.

The moment he knew she was in her room he reached for the phone. Now he could do the next thing he really wanted to do.

He dialled 1471.

'You were called at 21.37 by 07700 971 241. To return this call please dial 3.'

Danny didn't need to do ring-back: he knew the number. It was Anton Holt's. Anton was a football writer on the local paper, and Danny's friend. And he was the man who had helped Danny to solve the three major football crimes he'd been involved with in the last few months. The Sam Roberts kidnap. A Russian billionaire who was trying to kill England players. And Kofi's dodgy agent.

For a second he wondered why Holt would have been talking to Emily. Then he realized that he must have called while Emily was talking to whoever it was that was making her grin so broadly.

Now he wouldn't be able to find out who Emily had been talking to.

But he was pleased Anton had called. At 21.37 too. That would have been right after the game ended. Holt was in Madrid. At the match.

Danny would call him back tomorrow. He wanted Holt's angle on the game. And on the burglaries. Because Danny was really starting to feel like he was about to get his teeth into another football crime. One that struck right to the heart of his heroes. One that he was desperate to solve.

THE BURGLAR

The burglar had watched Danny with interest. Who was this boy waiting in the woods until he was seen off by the nine-thirty security shift? He can't have been a burglar too. Not a decent one. He'd made too many mistakes. Particularly being seen, the worst mistake of all.

The burglar assumed the boy was just a fan who had found out the address of his footballing hero and couldn't resist having a look. Albeit on a night he should have known the player was away. In Spain.

He smiled.

That was why *he* was here. He knew Didier François, the owner of this opulent house, was over a thousand miles away in Madrid. The burglar had even watched the first half on TV, before coming out. Seen City take the lead.

It was two in the morning now and he had been sitting in the tree for six hours.

Waiting.

He checked his watch. It was fifteen minutes since the last security patrol had started a circuit of the street. From high in the tree he could see the pair of guards work their way back to their office.

It was time.

He dropped down from the tree, branch to branch, five or six metres to the leafy floor.

He knew about the electric fence. It had taken him just five minutes to find its weakness on his first visit here a week ago. It was all very well having an electric fence round your gated community. But it was a mistake to build a shed right next to the fence, under the thick bough of a tree that hung perfectly above it.

He climbed that tree now and shimmied along the bough, stopping every ten seconds to listen. It was dark, so his sense of hearing was all the more important.

But there was no noise above the rustle and scuffle of the woods, sounds he knew were animals and birds from having spent hours among them.

Human noises were entirely different. Clumsy and out of tune with the wood.

His soft trainers made no sound when he dropped on to the roof of the shed. He spread his weight immediately, in case the shed had a weak roof. Although he knew from last time that it didn't.

He had done his homework. He'd found the same design of shed in a large DIY store near the City Stadium. He'd gone inside and checked the structure of the roof. Three two-inch-thick supports evenly spread. He even knew where to put his feet, so that he would be standing over the supports. It would carry his weight, no problem at all.

The burglar eased himself down from the shed, his heart picking up a pace.

Because this was the dangerous bit. Out in the open. If someone looked from the window of any of the houses now, they would see him. And he wouldn't *know* they'd seen him. Fatal.

He jogged across the lawn of the house he was going to break into tonight. Gazing in through the patio doors at the huge TV screen on the wall. The Ferrari coffee table he'd seen already in *HELLO!* magazine.

As he made his way for the cover of a two-metre-high wooden fence that surrounded the bins, his heart stopped. The garden suddenly flooded with light and he was exposed.

He ducked and hid behind a wheelie bin, catching his cheek on some branches. But he kept his back turned, so his face would not reflect light. His clothes were all as black as the shadows. His face stung where the branches had caught him.

But what was this? There *was* no security light. He'd seen cats and foxes move across this lawn and no light had come on. And he'd entered this way when he had broken into another house in the street earlier in the week and no light had triggered that time.

He sat perfectly still, not moving. Just listening. That was how he would deal with this surprise. No need to panic.

Then he heard it.

A rushing sound.

Water escaping down a pipe.

He looked up at the neighbouring house and saw a bathroom light go off. Now he was in darkness again.

The burglar smiled.

That had been no security light. Just someone next door with a weak bladder going to the toilet in the middle of the night. Just another person who was unaware that there was a man outside who was about to break into a Premier League footballer's house.

Getting into the house was easy. He couldn't believe that someone with so much money had such a cheap back door. Most of the houses he had done before had had thick wooden doors that were very difficult to get through.

Not this one.

He took out his Stanley knife and sliced through the white plastic of the door, towards the top of one of the lower panels. Then he pulled out the foam stuffing that insulated the door and cut through the plastic on the other side. These doors were cheap. He knew. He used to have one at home.

He checked to see if there was a key in the lock on the other side.

Unbelievably there was.

The burglar sighed. The owner of the house might be one of Europe's most intelligent foot-ballers, but he was an idiot when it came to household security.

Now the tricky bit.

The burglar alarm was on. He could hear the quiet beep-beep-beeping that meant he had up to sixty seconds to disable it.

He went to the cupboard where he knew it was. Through his binoculars, from the tree, he'd watched the player go to the alarm twice. And key in 2-3-1-1-8-4. A pathetic security code. The footballer's date of birth. Available to all on his fan website. Idiot.

Then the burglar's heart sank.

The little cupboard where the alarm keyboard was kept was locked. You could see the timer switch ticking away through a hole, but there was no access to the buttons to stop the alarm. The man looked around desperately for the key. Felt around the top of the cupboard.

He had thirty seconds left.

Nothing there.

His heart had picked up now. Beating too fast.

Fifteen seconds.

He even looked behind him. Panicking that someone was there.

That was when he knew that he was losing his cool. He had to focus.

He had ten seconds now.

How would he open this little cupboard? Or should he get out now? Run? Fail?

No way.

The burglar put his hand in his pocket again. He took out a small twenty-centimetre piece of iron. One end was curved like a crowbar.

He smashed it into the corner of the cupboard with all his force.

The cupboard disintegrated immediately, leaving the alarm keyboard exposed.

Then he tapped in the code – 2-3-1-1-8-4 – and the noise stopped.

And then he smiled.

The burglar knew that there was no one home. And no dog. So he went straight to the bedroom.

Bedrooms were where people kept their most prized things. Jewellery. Cash. Even guns.

He went through shelves, drawers, a blanket chest. When he found the cash in the sock drawer, he couldn't help smiling. The holder of a World Cup winner's medal keeping a wad of money in his sock drawer!

The burglar didn't bother looking for the medal. He knew that had to be in a bank vault. Even footballers couldn't be that stupid.

The cash was enough. A two- or three-centimetre-thick wad of twenty-pound notes. That had to be at least five grand. Maybe more.

And with such a haul he had no need to steal anything more.

He went back down the stairs. In the dark. Counting the steps he'd counted on the way up.

Now it was time for the bit he really enjoyed.

He went to the fridge and took out a beer. He flicked it open, the bottle top ricocheting across the kitchen work surface. He'd leave it there. It was his calling card.

He took his beer into the sitting room and drew the curtains across the patio doors. Then he found the remote control and flicked on the giant screen.

The channel on was Sky Sports News. Highlights of the night's games.

The burglar lay back on the sofa. This one was comfortable. The most comfortable so far. He put his feet up on the coffee table: the red Ferrari.

Then he sipped the beer and looked around the room. A basket full of PlayStation games. Hundreds of CDs and DVDs. A statue of an Egyptian cat or dog – he wasn't sure which. It was tasteless rubbish, he knew that much.

And then he sighed. This was how Premier

League players lived. And for the next five minutes he was a Premier League player.

Another swig of beer. Another sigh. Then a smile when he saw a footballer on the TV screen: the very player whose beer he was drinking now. The very player whose cash he had stuffed into his pocket.

And this was just the beginning.

THURSDAY

PHOTO FIT

Danny woke up the next morning when he heard his sister on the phone.

It was weird his parents being away. None of the usual noises of the house were there. His dad making tea first thing. His mum going off to work, flustered and grumpy. These were the noises he had heard all his life. Without them everything felt strange. Very strange.

He looked at the clock.

9.06 a.m.

That was even stranger. When was the last time he'd slept in past nine o'clock? He couldn't remember.

Danny lifted his head off his pillow to try to hear what his sister was saying. He was still suspicious of who she'd been on the phone to last night.

It was pretty obvious really: she had a new boyfriend.

This could often happen when she was seeing someone new. She'd be all cheery and nice. Before it all went wrong. Before the latest boy found out how mean Emily was.

But Danny had to admit to himself that he'd never seen her *this* cheery. It was more serious than normal. He just hoped she would stay happy at least until their parents got back.

Danny gave up trying to eavesdrop on her and flicked the radio on. He wanted to hear what City FC's manager had to say about the defeat at Real Madrid, to hear something positive, to make him believe they could get past the Spanish Champions: '. . . *police are investigating the burglary of another City FC player . . .*'

Danny sat up in his bed. He was wide awake now. The report went on: '. . . *yesterday night, while the French international Didier François was playing in City's defeat at Real Madrid, his house was broken into and items were stolen. A thirty-seven-year-old security guard was arrested at the scene, but was later released without charge.*

'*The player, who is returning from Spain today,*

has written on his Twitter site of his shock. "But at least there was nobody of my family at home," he posted.

'This is a reference to the previous burglary of City player Juan Goytisolo, whose wife and two children were forced to flee their home when burgled during City's last European away game in Marseille.

'Police say they have a lead. A young man or boy, aged between fourteen and eighteen, was seen in the area of François's property. They are putting together a photo fit that will be published in the* Evening Post *later today . . .'*

Danny flicked off the radio once the reporter went on to cover other news stories.

What was this?

He felt as if his blood had stopped running through his veins.

François burgled?

A boy aged between fourteen and eighteen seen near the player's house?

A photo fit going to be published?

What if it was *him*? What if the security guard had thought *he* was the burglar? He could easily think that. Had the house been burgled by the time Danny arrived?

Danny's mind was swimming with fears.

Whether they thought he was involved in the burglary or not, he had been there on the night the player had been robbed. So he had been near the burglar. Possibly.

Danny cursed. That was the other thing. If he had been close to the burglar, he had been close to solving the crimes.

On the other hand, if he had been close to the burglar, he had also been close to danger.

And what about the security guard mentioned on the radio report? Why had he been arrested? Then released? Was it the same security guard he had seen in the woods?

A knock on the door shocked Danny out of his thoughts.

'Morning.' It was Emily. Carrying a tray and smiling sweetly. 'Breakfast?'

What was this? Breakfast in bed?

He knew something very strange was going on now. Danny spoke calmly. 'What's the matter?' he asked.

'Nothing. What do you mean?' Emily smiled again. 'I'm just looking after you, now Mum and Dad are away.'

'Do you want something?' Danny said, persisting. He was confused. He couldn't work out why his sister, who was normally horrible to him, was now being nicer than nice. Too nice. Even if she was all loved up.

He watched her make a mock-offended face, then smile again.

'I'm looking after you,' she said.

He sat up and she placed the tray on his legs. Cereal. Croissant. Juice. Tea. Yoghurt.

Danny wished he wasn't so tense about the burglaries. He would have really enjoyed this normally. It might never happen again.

'Thanks,' Danny said.

'You're welcome,' Emily replied, making to leave.

'Who phoned?' Danny asked quickly, trying to catch his sister off guard. In one of the crime series he read to his dad, the detective always asked a key question of one of his suspects when they were just about to leave the room, when they thought they'd got away with it.

Emily stopped, her face turned away from him.

'No one,' she said.

'No one?'

'Just a friend, I mean.'

Danny nodded as he watched his sister disappear out of the door.

After he'd eaten breakfast in bed, Danny lay there, trying to work out what to do if the photo fit was of him. What if it was? What did that mean? Would someone he knew call the police and say it was Danny, then the police would come round? Or would one of the police who arrested him a few weeks before identify him and call him into the police station? Or would it look like any one of a hundred boys from the city, and would people laugh and say it looked like him, not realizing it *was* him?

Danny reached for his mobile. He'd had three texts already that morning.

One was from Charlotte. His friend.

Wanna meet? C x

That meant Charlotte was free. He'd go and see her at some point. They'd seen a lot of each other this holiday. Especially as his best mate, Paul, was away with his mum and dad.

The next text was from Anton:

Did you see match? City were good.

Danny resolved to call Holt later. He must want
to talk.

The third text was from Kofi. It was a reply
to his email from the night before.

**Yes. I am free later today. Would you
like to meet this afternoon, Danny?
From Kofi**

Danny jumped out of bed. He had to get on. Call
Holt. Meet Kofi and Charlotte.

But most of all, he had to find out if the photo
fit about to be plastered across town was of him.

THE SUSPECT

'Hello?'

'Anton. It's Danny.'

Danny had decided to call his journalist friend first.

'All right, Danny. How's it going?'

'Fine.'

Danny waited for Holt to speak. To see why he'd called last night. But there was a silence. The kind of silence that you can't quite say why it's happening and you feel uncomfortable and you know the person on the other end of the line is feeling uncomfortable too.

Eventually Holt filled it.

'So, er . . . did you see the game last night?'

'No, I was out,' Danny said, wondering if he should tell Holt about his surveillance the night before. But what he really wanted to talk about was the photo fit. It was worrying him. A lot. And he'd not been able to talk to anyone about it.

'Yeah?'

'Yeah,' Danny said, lost for words. He'd expected Holt to lead the conversation.

More silence. Danny wondered what was going on. He and Holt had always been so easy with each other, ever since they'd started solving crimes between them.

Danny decided to fill the silence this time. 'You called last night?' he said. 'I was just calling you back.'

'Did I? Oh . . . oh . . . yes.'

Danny said nothing. This was getting weirder.

'Yeah,' Holt went on. 'I wanted to fill you in on the game. It was pretty good. Madrid look vulnerable in some ways. I think City could get behind them.'

Why was Holt talking like this? Danny wondered. Like he was reading out one of his match reports?

And he realized that he must be bothering Holt. He was a busy man, after all.

'Listen,' Danny cut in. 'I'll talk to you later. I've some stuff to do.'

'Like what?' Holt asked.

'This and that.' Danny smiled.

'Catching burglars?'

Danny's smile broadened. This was more like it.

'Maybe,' he said. And he wondered if he should mention the photo fit: to see what Holt knew.

'Then I've got something for you,' Holt said. 'To do with the burglaries.'

Danny waited. Now they were talking. He wondered why their conversation had started so weirdly. Maybe it was him. Maybe he'd spent too long with his sister.

'You wanna know?' Holt asked.

'Yes,' Danny said.

'The burglaries. I've got a suspect.'

'Who?'

'Do you remember Paul Wire?'

'The City player? Yeah, of course.'

'Do you know about his dodgy recent past?'

Danny did. Wire had been a great player. But he'd fallen apart once he'd stopped playing. He'd gambled a lot of money away. Left his wife and kids. And had been convicted of drugs offences, even going to prison, refusing to name the people the police thought had really done the crimes.

'Well, he's out of prison,' Holt said.

'So?'

'And he's back with his old mates.'

'Right,' Danny said. 'Do you think he's involved?'

'Another ex-player told me something,' Holt said. 'I can't say who. Or what he said. But he's someone I really trust.'

'Do you want me to check it out?'

'Would you be careful?'

'Of course.'

'I mean really careful. Only watching. You mustn't do anything.'

'I'll be fine. I've done it before. I won't take risks.'

Danny heard Holt laugh. 'So you won't end up being kidnapped or anything?'

'Not me,' Danny said.

'OK.' Holt paused. 'But you're just to watch – from a distance.'

'Sure.'

Danny suddenly felt aware of a silence behind him. He looked round. Emily was standing in the doorway. Smiling.

Danny smiled back and walked past her into the front room, shutting the door.

He lowered his voice. 'What do I do then?'

Holt paused. 'Why have you started whispering?'

'My sister's listening.'

'Right,' Holt said.

'So?'

'What?'

'What do I do?'

'About your sister?'

Danny put his hand to his head. Holt was going funny on him again. What had he said now?

Then Holt started talking. 'Oh right, yeah – Wire drinks at the Precinct. The pub in town.'

'I know it,' Danny said, relieved they seemed to be back on track. 'It's opposite a Starbucks.'

'Don't go in it,' Holt said.

'I'm fourteen.'

'Yeah,' Holt conceded. 'I forget that sometimes. Anyway, the Starbucks opposite. If you want to sit in there and watch who goes in and out, who Wire is talking to –'

'How will I see into the pub?' Danny interrupted.

'Wire smokes,' Holt answered. 'He spends half his time on the doorstep, talking to his mates.'

Danny nodded.

'Just watch,' Holt went on. 'He's in there eleven a.m. to six p.m. most days. Don't take photos. Have as many drinks as you like. And eat. Keep your receipts. It's on me. Have you got some money?'

'In my savings account, yeah.'

'Take out fifty quid. I'll pay you it back next time I see you.'

'Great,' Danny said. 'So what am I looking for?'

'I'll email you some photos of men. Some of the city's best-known fences. They get rid of stolen gear. Sell it on. If he's seen with them, then it suggests he has stolen gear to get rid of.'

'Can I ask you about something else?' Danny said. It was the right time to mention the photo fit. He needed to talk to Holt. Not to see what he could do to help, but just to get Holt's take on it. He was finding it hard to think about anything with it hanging over him.

'Sure. What?'

Danny was about to speak, but then he heard his sister behind the door. Shifting her feet.

'Forget it,' Danny said. 'It can wait.'

'OK,' Holt replied. 'See you.'

As soon as Danny put the phone down, Emily came in.

'Who was that?' she asked.

'No one,' Danny said.

'Who?' she persisted, her face changing slightly, showing the real Emily, not this smiling and nice sister she had become recently.

'Charlotte,' Danny said.

Emily shook her head. 'No, it wasn't.'

'Well, who do you think it was?'

Emily said nothing. Then she coughed and smiled her new smile. 'Drink?' she said. 'Cup of tea?'

'No thanks,' Danny said. 'I'm going out.'

Once he was ready to go – and he had printed off the pictures of suspects Holt had sent him – he called Kofi. They agreed to meet at the Star-bucks.

Exactly where Danny wanted to be. Right now.

IAN MILLS

Danny was surprised to see another boy arrive with Kofi.

He had been sitting in the Starbucks opposite the pub for half an hour. And he'd spotted nothing unusual. No ex-players. No one smoking in the doorway. None of the men in the four photos Holt had emailed him. The coffee shop had been quiet too. People talking, tapping keyboards over a cold cappuccino. Non-customers, sneaking in to use the toilet.

But now it was lunchtime. And getting busier.

Kofi waved and smiled openly when he saw Danny. Then he and the other lad picked their way through the chaos of tables to the window area where Danny had set himself up.

'This is Ian Mills,' Kofi said, facing Danny, the other boy behind him. He had a shaved head, suntanned face and was wearing sunglasses on an overcast day. Something in Kofi's eyes was telling Danny he was sorry that Ian had come, that he hadn't actually invited him. No words passed between them. But Danny knew it.

'Hi Ian. I'm Danny.'

Ian nodded. And Danny noticed he had faint scratches on his cheek. Like he'd been in a fight or something.

'Would you like a drink, Danny?' Kofi asked.

'No thanks,' Danny said, glancing at his unfinished coffee.

'Macchiato for me, Kofi,' Ian said, making to sit. Then he peeled twenty pounds off a huge handful of notes and handed it to Kofi. 'On me,' he said.

And Kofi was off, heading for the counter, leaving Danny to work out who Ian was and what he should say to him.

But it was Ian who started asking the questions.

'You look familiar,' Ian said. 'Have I seen you before?'

Danny shook his head, smiling. But deep down his stomach contracted. Had Ian seen the photo

48

fit that was supposed to be in the paper today? Maybe it did look like Danny.

'Are you a fan?' Ian went on, once he'd stopped looking out of the window at two girls who were walking past.

'A City fan? Yeah,' Danny replied.

'A fan of Kofi,' Ian said, 'I mean, like a – you know – hanger-on?'

Danny wondered if he'd heard Ian right. It was an odd question. 'We're more like friends,' he said.

Ian looked surprised. Then he said, 'I've been on City's books since I was nine.'

Danny nodded. A player. This was more interesting. 'Do you train with Kofi?' he asked.

'Not any more,' Ian said. 'I'm considering my options. Might have a trial at Forza FC. They're an Italian club. They're going to be huge.'

This must mean that Ian had been let go by City, that the club didn't think he was good enough. There was no way he'd be talking about another club like this otherwise. But Danny didn't push. He had no idea what being released by a football club would feel like – so he left it.

Ian went on. 'They're playing their first year in the Champions League this season.'

'Yes, I've seen them,' Danny said. He wanted to say more. Say that he knew all about the Champions League, thanks very much. But Ian was gazing out of the window at a truck reversing. Its beep-beep-beeping filling the café as someone opened the door to leave.

Danny decided to keep his mouth shut. He wished Kofi would come back with the drinks.

'So how do you know Kofi then, if . . . you're not at City?' Ian asked.

Danny smiled again. Ian was making some pretty strange assumptions. That footballers didn't know real people like him. That Kofi had to get something out of Danny for him to bother being friends with him. Maybe it was true for Ian, Danny thought. He didn't really know what to say in response.

Mercifully Kofi arrived then with a cup of black tea for himself and a funny-looking coffee for Ian.

'How is school?' Kofi asked. 'What are you learning?'

'School!' Ian broke in. 'You're still at school?' He sounded shocked.

'I'm fourteen,' Danny said.

'I pretty much left school when I was *thirteen*,'

Ian interrupted. 'Once I was at City and I knew I was going to be a pro footballer.'

Danny ignored him and just answered Kofi's question. 'English. Maths. That sort of thing.'

'Boring,' said Ian, watching a young woman who was leaning against a lamppost, laughing into a mobile phone.

Danny looked down at his drink. He was surprised Ian wasn't making him feel more angry. In fact, he was just amused at how ridiculous Ian seemed.

'City have offered to put me on an educational course,' Kofi said. 'At night school.'

'Great,' Danny said.

'Waste of time,' Ian said, still not even bothering to turn away from the window to speak to them properly. 'You don't need to pass exams to make money. Footballer or not.'

Kofi made a little shrugging gesture to Danny.

Danny glanced at his watch, hoping Ian would leave.

'I want to show you my new home,' Kofi said to Danny after a moment.

'You've moved in?' Danny said, noticing Ian was now looking more interested in the conversation.

'Yes. And I have some good things. A stereo. A TV. Lots of new things. I have never had these things before. City have given them to me.'

'That's great,' Danny said, looking at Ian again, wondering if he was going to speak. The boy was suddenly paying attention and had a black look on his face. Like he was jealous.

'I bet they're the best money can buy too,' Ian spat.

'Yes. They are very good,' Kofi said cheerfully.

Ian glared out of the window again as Kofi wrote something on a notepad.

'This is my new home address,' Kofi said, passing a piece of paper across Ian to Danny.

Danny noticed Ian look at it and sneer.

Half an hour later they were still in Starbucks. It had been a strange thirty minutes. Danny reflected that sometimes it was hard to talk to a friend when there was somebody new there. But now the subject had changed to the City FC burglaries. And that, at least, interested Danny. Especially as Ian was still showing off about what he knew.

'That's five of the lads burgled,' he was saying.

Danny nodded.

'And do you know where they all live?' Ian carried on.

'No,' Danny said, neither wishing to incriminate himself nor stop Ian telling him.

'Baird lives in a gated street in Fixham. The village north of the city. It's as exclusive as you can get. Sabella and Butterworth live in flats in that tower block by the canal. The one that's a Hilton hotel on the first thirty floors, then penthouses above. They live there.'

Ian was delivering all this information as if he knew all the players personally and had been to their houses. But Danny was pleased he was boasting. He hadn't known all this. It was a huge help.

'Then it was Hawley earlier this week, and François last night. Another gated street. With security. And all while they were playing away. In Europe.'

Danny nodded again.

'Through the trees and in through the back door,' Ian went on, laughing.

Danny nodded a third time. That was spot on. His mind was starting to go over how much Ian knew, the implications. But then he noticed that Ian had eventually stopped speaking and was gazing out of the window. Again.

'Look at that,' he said, pointing at a girl. 'Nice. She's waving at me.'

Danny looked. The girl *was* waving. But not at Ian. She was waving at Danny – and at Kofi. And that was because it was Charlotte.

'She's coming in,' Ian said, half standing with excitement. 'She must be a fan.'

'Ian,' Kofi said calmly. 'That is Charlotte. She is a friend of Danny.'

Ian nodded, but Danny couldn't tell if he'd taken in what Kofi had said.

They all watched Charlotte as she walked towards them.

'Hello,' Ian said to Charlotte.

Charlotte smiled as she approached the table, then looked at Danny, brushing a strand of hair away from her eyes.

'I can't stop,' she said. 'I'm meeting my mum.'

'Sit here,' Ian said, patting his chair. 'I've kept it warm for you.'

Charlotte smiled again, but Danny saw the *Who on earth is this?* look in her eyes.

'You a schoolgirl too?' said Ian, looking at Charlotte, then at Danny.

'Yes,' Charlotte replied in a cool voice, dead-pan.

'I'm Ian Mills. I'm a . . . footballer.'

'You were,' Danny said, under his breath, watching Ian drop a set of car keys on the table, a large Porsche logo on one of them.

'You don't look like a footballer,' Charlotte said, ignoring the keys. Then she turned to Kofi. 'How are you doing, Kofi? Are they looking after you?'

'Yes, thank you. I am very happy.'

Danny had to cough to stop himself laughing. Charlotte had stopped Ian boasting with one remark. Genius.

Charlotte only stayed for another five minutes – she seemed to notice the tension round the table.

'I have to go,' she said. 'See you tomorrow, Danny?'

Danny nodded. Then Charlotte hugged Kofi. 'It's lovely to see you,' she said.

'It is lovely to see you too,' Kofi said, grinning.

Ian was leaning back in his seat. He had his mobile phone in his hand. Then, after having said nothing for three minutes, he said, 'Can I have your number?' looking at Charlotte.

Charlotte smiled. 'No,' she said. 'You can't.'

CAUGHT IN THE ACT

The second house that week looked easy.

It was in the middle of nowhere. A converted barn in the countryside, but on a main road. And that helped: it meant that when one of the heavier lorries came past he could make noise without worrying about being overheard.

The burglar had been watching the house all afternoon, after he'd sorted out some business in the city centre. No one had come in or out all afternoon. And, since it had gone dark, no lights had come on. Not even lights on timers.

This *was* going to be easy. The last one had been harder. Guards. Fences. Alarms. Boys watching in the woods. This was a piece of cake. He smiled. He'd never done two players' houses, one night after the other. But he was feeling good. He wanted to do more. Find more money.

And – he had to admit it to himself – it excited him. Being in the house of a professional foot-baller. The *empty* house of a professional footballer. Taking things off them. That was the best bit.

He felt the familiar anger return. Why should they have all the fame and the money? Half of the players at City FC were rubbish. There were hundreds of boys who didn't make it who were better than the City FC players. The ones who made it were just lucky. He hated to see the young players being interviewed on TV, hated seeing their names on the list of the England under-eighteens squad. They had all the lime-light. Sometimes he wished he was the famous one. Famous for robbing their houses. He occasionally fantasised about it. Being on TV dragged from a house, all the cameras on him.

Anyway, this latest house was going to be no problem. And the burglar knew whose house it was. Alex Finn. City's keeper. England's number one goalie.

What would he find here?

Medals?

England caps?

Keepers' gloves?

Or cash. Because that's what he really wanted. Money.

He liked money. It made up for the things that had started to go wrong in his life. It could buy him things. Things he wanted.

But to business. Getting in.

He took great pleasure in smashing the front door down. You never got the chance to do this normally. Houses were usually overlooked by other houses. So you never knew who was watching you. But today – as he had already decided – he could do it. There wasn't another house nearby. No problem.

He ran at the door from three metres away and kicked hard.

The door splintered around the lock. Almost opening first time. He kicked at the door again. It swung open.

This was so easy. The door was actually rotting, so it came apart with no trouble at all. He couldn't believe his luck – Alex Finn should be able to afford to have the same doors they had at Fort Knox.

The burglar bounced into the house, surfing on the adrenalin that was streaming through his blood.

He wouldn't bother to disable the alarm. The house was a good sixteen miles away from the nearest police station. He had checked on Google. You could see where all the police stations were. He knew he had at least fifteen minutes to search the property.

What next?

He had to open the back door. Then he could escape if someone came home while he was in the house.

Then what?

The bedroom. Always start in the bedroom. He went up a narrow flight of stairs. The house was all old beams and wooden floors. Not very cosy. Quite cold. There were clothes lying on the landing floor.

He went into a large bedroom with mirrors along one wall.

It was a mess. More clothes all over the place. Old newspapers. Half-drunk cups of tea.

This player was a slob, he thought. He couldn't even keep his house clean. It wasn't like he didn't have the time. Footballers had loads of time. They only had to train for a few hours a day.

Focus, he told himself. *Focus*. He headed for a chest of drawers. He'd start there. He turned several of the drawers over, tipping their contents on to the bed.

Nothing. Just T-shirts, jogging bottoms.

He pulled several baskets out of the main cupboard and tipped them on the bed too.

Nothing. Socks. Pants.

Now what? Another room. He made to go and find the second bedroom. But then he saw it. A black briefcase. At the back of the cupboard. On a high shelf.

He pulled it down. Something told him this was what he was looking for. It had a combination lock. He could either take this away and open it later or smash it to pieces with his foot now.

He'd do the latter. He liked smashing things in footballers' houses. They deserved it.

He placed the briefcase on the floor and leaned on the wall, his foot poised above it.

And then he saw the lights. A pair of headlights sweeping across the driveway, coming from the main road.

Adrenalin immediately ran through his blood.

He left the unopened case and ran for the stairs.

The stairs would take him to the doorway

where whoever was in the car would be coming in. But that was his only choice.

He ran to the landing, hearing a car door opening.

Down the stairs.

As he hit the bottom steps, holding on to the banister to swing round so he could run to the back door, he saw the figure.

Alex Finn.

Alex Finn, a big man. In the doorway. His heart felt as if it was about to burst out through his throat. He felt sick.

But he had to run.

'Get here, you little . . .'

But he was already in the kitchen at the back of the house. Running. He felt like he was flying.

'Leave it, Alex!' Another voice. A woman's voice.

He burst out through the back door, hurting his hand as he did, catching it on the lock.

Then he ran again. Through a garden. Across lawns. Leaping a pond. Over a wall. Then he was in a field. It was dark. He wasn't sure what he was doing now. Just run – he knew that was what he should do. That was what the voice in his head was telling him.

So he ran. And ran. And ran. Until he couldn't run any more. Until he was forced to slump under a tree. Until he felt like he was going to die of an exploding chest.

And it was only then that he realized that his sleeve was drenched with blood from his cut hand.

FRIDAY

DETECTIVE AGAIN

As Danny came down the stairs he smelled bacon.

Bacon? At home?

His mum hated bacon because it stank the house out. They were never allowed it, however much Danny loved a bacon sandwich.

He pushed the kitchen door open. And there was Emily. Sitting at the table in the window.

'I heard you get up,' she said. 'I was going to bring you a bacon sandwich.'

'Thanks,' Danny said.

'Do you want it now?' his sister went on.

'Go on then.'

Emily smiled, then got up from the table and went towards the frying pan.

Danny gazed out of the window and wondered if he should say something. He and Emily had never done small talk. But Danny was aware that she was still trying to be nice, for whatever reason. And that maybe he should be nice back. It was worth a go. Maybe this was a chance for them to get on better.

The thought came into his head that he should tell her about the photo fit. It was still pressing on his mind that he could get into a lot of trouble. But it would be madness telling her. Danny realized he must be missing his dad. It was the kind of thing he might be able to talk to his dad about.

If his dad was here he could even tell him about the reconnaissance he was doing for Holt. His dad might have some good ideas to help him. Or at least offer him moral support.

'What are you doing today?' Danny asked, deciding to play it safe.

Emily turned with a huge grin. 'Seeing a friend,' she beamed.

The boy. Danny knew that much.

'Is he nice?' he asked, hoping she'd take it the right way.

'He is.' More grinning.

Oh no, Danny thought. *This is serious.* Whoever this boy was he was having a good effect on Emily.

They sat and ate. Emily passed Danny the ketchup without him having to ask.

And then she asked, 'Do you ever think about leaving home?'

Danny shook his head, his mouth full of bread and bacon. What was this?

'Imagine. Bacon sandwiches every day. Watching what you want on TV. A bathroom to yourself.'

Danny shrugged. 'I suppose you'll be going to leave soon anyway,' he said. 'If you go to university.'

'If!' Emily said.

Danny swallowed his next piece of sandwich before he spoke.

'If?'

'Yeah. If . . . Maybe I want to stay here now.'

Danny wondered what their mum and dad would say to this. That Emily didn't want to do what they had always intended her to do. Get a full education, they called it. They expected it of Danny too. And he was fine about that. He knew he was going to university. And he knew what he was going to study.

Criminology.

'What about you?' Emily said.

Danny considered opening up to her, saying he wanted to study crime, that that was his passion. But then she changed the subject.

'What are you doing today? Seeing that journalist friend of yours?'

'Anton?'

'Yeah. Anton.'

Danny shrugged. 'I doubt it. He's busy.'

But Emily was away grinning at nothing again.

Upstairs, in his bedroom, Danny got a box down from the top shelf.

It was the box containing the things he had had on his wall until a few weeks before. The things he used to help him solve crimes. The things his mum and dad had asked him to take off his wall because they were worried he was taking his criminal investigations too far. That he was putting his life at risk. Like the time he'd been caught trespassing by the police while watching the City FC stadium. And the time he'd been shot at by Kofi's dodgy football agent.

Everything was there.

A large map of the city, dotted with coloured stickers showing where certain crimes had taken place. Three notebooks, two of them full. Four scrapbooks full of cuttings from newspapers. All about crimes. Then some more interesting things. A wind-up torch. A camera. A balaclava.

His detective kit. His football detective kit.

Danny spread the map out on the floor. He immediately felt happier than he had for weeks. He missed his map. He had, in the past, spent hours just staring at the map, looking at where burglaries had taken place, or bank jobs, post office raids. All the crimes of the city over the last year or more were there, things he'd read about in the paper.

Danny took out a sheet of stickers. He needed a new coloured sticker to mark the five footballer burglaries. He chose blue. He'd not used blue ones yet.

He pulled a list out of his pocket: details of the burglaries – according to Ian Mills the day before.

He had one of the burgled footballers' addresses. The one he'd been at Wednesday night. Everyone knew that Didier François lived there. But he hadn't known the addresses of the other burgled players. Until Ian Mills had told him. And he'd also told him where some of the other players lived.

He stuck them on the map. Just like he'd read in a book. A detective novel he'd read to his dad. The detective – an amateur like Danny – had plotted out crimes on a map and solved it.

Now Danny had to choose a footballer's house that had not been burgled yet. But who would it be? He'd probably get it wrong.

But what else could he do? A proper detective would do more than just waiting all day to go and watch a house that may or may not be going to be burgled.

Then what Anton said came into his mind again. About who could be doing it. Maybe he should start there and not with houses. Paul Wire. The ex-City player who he had a lead on.

Could it be him?

It could. Maybe. Danny had read a lot of footballer autobiographies. Most were ordinary, about how players had been picked up by a professional club when they were young. How they'd become successful. Who their best friends in the game were. Nothing controversial. All pretty much the same.

But some were different. Players whose careers had fallen apart, who had got involved with drink and drugs. Some who had ended up in prison. He remembered one player who had gone from a Premier League winning team to stealing alcohol from a supermarket within three years. Another who had been sent to prison for killing a family in a car accident, while drunk.

So it *could* happen. It *was* possible. An ex-City FC player may well now be involved in burglary and trying to sell on the rewards of his robberies.

Maybe he *should* go and watch for Wire again. Not go to some random house. It made sense. And it was as close to a lead as he could get. Just go and watch. He should have done it for longer yesterday. This was the only answer.

Danny stood up. That was what he'd do. Watch, gather evidence. Not get distracted by idiotic ex-footballers like Ian Mills.

He pulled his hoody on. Then went to his computer to check his emails.

But he never got as far as his emails.

His home page was BBC Football news. He had it like that so he could always see the latest football news as soon as possible.

He read the headline:

SIXTH CITY FC PLAYER ROBBED

Alex Finn disturbs burglar in his £3M converted barn

Danny ran down the stairs, feeling – he had to be honest with himself – excited that there had been another crime. He shouted goodbye to his sister, then took out his mobile phone. Now was the time to go looking for Wire. If he was going to catch him out it had to be now.

And he knew that this was getting serious. Very serious.

STASH

Danny walked swiftly down his road, towards the bus stop.

He called Anton on the way. But the reply was just a message: *Hi, this is Anton Holt at the* Evening Post. *Please leave a message after the bleep.*

'It's Danny. I just heard about Finn on the radio. I expect you're covering it. I'm going to the Starbucks to see if Wire comes to the pub. Call me if you can.'

Danny slipped his mobile into his pocket. He looked around. It was a nice day. Dry, mild, clear sky. A good day for a kickabout. Sometimes he thought that maybe he should be doing things like that again. Not sitting drinking coffee and watching pub doorways.

Then an idea came to Danny.

Charlotte.

Maybe she'd come with him. He wanted to see her on his own without the likes of Ian Mills around. She would be good at just watching. She knew about his football detecting. She had helped him more than once. Maybe he was starting to think of her as a partner.

He found her number and dialled. She picked up after one ring.

'Hi Danny.' She sounded enthusiastic. A good sign.

'Do you fancy helping me solve another crime?' he asked, in a mock-mysterious voice.

Charlotte said nothing. Not a good sign.

'Don't worry. No one will shoot at us this time.'

There was a long silence. He waited. Until he heard Charlotte laugh. 'OK,' she said.

And that was it. She agreed to meet him. At Starbucks. In an hour.

The city centre was quiet. Not many shoppers. No one out on their lunch break yet. It was cloudy and cold now. A sudden change in the weather. Danny was glad to be inside where it was warm.

'So what are we looking for?'

Danny glanced at the door of the pub opposite Starbucks. Then back to Charlotte. She was wearing her hair differently today. Not just hanging down but tied back in two pigtails. Danny wondered why he'd suddenly started noticing her hairstyle.

'An ex-City player,' he said. 'Paul Wire. He was a footballer, then he got involved in lots of dodgy stuff. Anton's had a tip that Wire's involved in the footballers being burgled. And, because there was a footballer robbed yesterday, this is a good day to see if he is seeing his fence, or whatever.'

'Do you think it's him?' Charlotte asked.

'I don't know. But there are no other leads and Anton said it was a solid tip.'

'So who gave him the tip?'

'He wouldn't tell me. An ex-player. That's all he said.'

Danny got out the photos of Wire's possible associates.

'These are the men he might be seen with,' Danny said, quieter now. 'Anton sent me the photos.'

Charlotte studied them, then, after a moment,

leaned towards Danny, pausing while the coffee machine was making its racket.

'How are things at home?' Charlotte asked.

'With Emily?' Danny asked, wondering what she meant.

'Yeah. Is she still being nice?'

Danny smiled. 'Yeah.'

'Maybe she's grown up?'

'Maybe,' Danny answered. 'She has started wearing these funny scarves. Like she thinks she's an adult all of a sudden.'

'I bet she's got an older boyfriend,' Charlotte said.

'You reckon?'

'I know it. It's obvious.'

Danny looked at Charlotte and nodded. Then his eyes returned to the door of the pub. And there he was.

Paul Wire.

Lighting a cigarette.

'Don't look,' Danny said to Charlotte, 'but that's him.'

Charlotte looked.

Danny rolled his eyes.

'He's not very fit, is he?'

'What do you mean?' Danny asked.

'He's not very good looking. I thought footballers were supposed to be good looking.'

For some reason this remark made Danny feel
uneasy. He didn't know what to say.

Charlotte went on, unaware. 'And now he's
talking to someone.'

Danny looked. She was right. Wire was talking
to a man who had stopped in the street. He was
tall, muscular and young, making Wire look
smaller and older. They shook hands. Danny
looked more closely. The man was familiar.

'The pictures,' Danny said to himself. He
pointed at Holt's set of images of known criminals. He scanned the four faces. And there he
was. A dark-haired man with a moustache.
Francis Graham.

As he studied the picture, Danny heard three
or four clicks.

He looked at Charlotte. She was holding a
camera to the window. She'd got it all.

'I thought while you were admiring the view,
I'd get some evidence.' She smiled.

The two of them stared at the empty pub door
for a moment. Wire and Graham had gone in.

'That's one of the men that Holt said he might
be with.'

'Who?'

Danny handed Charlotte the picture.

'Francis Graham,' she said. 'What is he a criminal for? I mean, what did he do?'

'He sells on stolen goods,' Danny said. 'Anton reckons.'

Charlotte nodded. 'So what now?'

Danny paused. Then he said, 'We go in.'

'Into the pub?'

'Yeah.'

'But they'll spot us a mile off. We're underage.'

Danny's mind started working. 'We say we're looking for our dad, or something. They'll let us in for a minute. Then we might get a glimpse of Wire and the other guy.'

'Why?'

'Because we might be about to gather evidence to help solve a massive crime. If he's going to be handing over stolen things, it'll be now.'

Danny didn't expect Charlotte to go for this reasoning. It was risky. Why would she want to go into a seedy pub after two dodgy men?

But suddenly Charlotte was on her feet. She'd drained her drink. 'Come on then,' she said.

And there was no time to think of any reasons why not to go in. It was now. Or never.

They walked confidently into the pub. That was the only way. They would say that they were looking for their dad, that they were used to trying to find him in pubs. It had to look convincing.

The pub was dark, with low-wattage bulbs barely illuminating the brown carpet and yellow walls. The bar ran back into the pub, rows and rows of drinks in bottles and cans behind the tills. There was a girl behind the bar, cleaning glasses, long blonde hair tied back, heavy make-up. She looked not much older than Charlotte. Danny wondered if she was eighteen at all. As he looked at her, Danny could feel Charlotte's eyes on him.

Then the barmaid turned round.

'Is Jim Watts in here?' Charlotte said loudly. 'He's bald. He wears a black leather jacket.'

'No,' the girl said, glancing from Charlotte to Danny, smiling at Danny.

'Can we look?' Charlotte said in a voice Danny didn't recognize. She was acting the part well.

The girl shrugged.

Then Danny felt Charlotte grab his hand and they were walking down to the far end of the pub.

It was a long dingy place. And it smelled. Stale. Sour. Bad.

There was no one in the main part of the pub. And when they reached the bottom end, where there were two toilet doors, they realized it was empty.

'So where did they go?' Danny asked. Wire and the other man had vanished.

Charlotte shrugged.

'You check the Gents,' Charlotte suggested. 'And I'll check the Ladies.'

Danny nodded and went into the Gents. They stank too. He looked around. Three urinals. Two toilets in cubicles. Both empty. A wad of hand towels on the floor in a pool of water.

Wire and the other man must have disappeared. Or they had gone behind the bar. Maybe into a back room, through a door Danny hadn't seen.

He left the toilets and stood outside the Ladies.

As he stood waiting for Charlotte, Danny noticed the girl behind the bar looking at him, smiling. He smiled back, then felt a grab at his hand.

Charlotte.

'Don't speak,' she said, dragging him along. Out of the pub and into the street.

Once they were through the heavy swing door, they were hit by a wall of light. It was bright, so bright it hurt Danny's eyes. Charlotte carried on dragging him until they were on the other side of the street, standing in an unused doorway.

'What's going on?' Danny asked.

'They were in there,' Charlotte said. 'In the Ladies.'

'What?'

'The two men.' Charlotte was breathless. 'Wire and whatshisname.'

'Doing what?' Danny couldn't believe it.

'I went into one cubicle and they were in the next one. One of them was stood on the toilet. Messing with the ceiling tiles. He looked down at me.'

It was then that Danny saw Wire come out of the pub.

'It's him,' Danny said.

Charlotte looked. Danny could see panic in her eyes.

Because Paul Wire and Francis Graham were pointing at them. And moving their way.

CLOCKED

'Come on,' Danny said.

Charlotte seemed paralysed, just standing and looking at the two men.

'What?' she said.

'We need to go.' Danny grabbed Charlotte's hand. This time he was leading her.

They ran mid-pace out on to the main shopping street. Danny noticed a couple of people looking at them. He knew they looked odd, running through a city centre. When he saw people running in town he always suspected they were shoplifters making an escape. Maybe that was what people thought of him and Charlotte.

He looked back to see if he could spot Wire and Graham. But they weren't in pursuit.

Danny slowed down and realized he was still holding Charlotte's hand. He let it go.

'Are they coming?' Charlotte asked, breathless.

'No.'

'Were they following us?'

'I thought so. But . . . maybe not. We should keep going though. We need to get further away. Just in case.'

They carried on down the high street, past the shops, then up a side road. There were fewer people in this part of town. It was strangely quiet. Danny looked behind him again. In case they *were* being followed. But he could see no sign of Wire and Graham.

Danny watched Charlotte pull her hair out of its pigtails.

'Disguise,' she said, smiling.

'Tell me what they did again?' Danny said. He'd been trying to work out why they'd been in the Ladies' toilet.

Charlotte paused for a second before speaking.

'Wire was standing on the toilet and the other one was on the floor. Wire was moving one of the ceiling tiles. I mean . . . why would they do that?'

'Drugs,' Danny said.

'What?'

'They were hiding drugs.'

'How's that?' Charlotte said, sounding sceptical.

'I read about it,' Danny said. 'A drug dealer used to keep all his drugs in a toilet at a department store. He kept it there and came back for it every day.'

'And?'

'And he got found out.'

Charlotte nodded. 'So does that mean Wire isn't your burglar?'

'No. It just means he might be dealing drugs. Or something,' Danny answered. 'He might be the burglar too.'

They walked on. Towards the station. Now they were nearer the bus and train stations, things were busier. There were more people in black coats carrying black bags. And more women with pushchairs.

'Shall we go for a sandwich?' Charlotte asked after a couple of minutes' walking.

'OK.'

They each bought a sandwich at the station and sat on a couple of spare seats, watching people coming out from the barriers, running to get their trains, being met by people they knew.

'What are you going to do now?' Charlotte asked.

Danny didn't reply.

'Danny?'

But Danny wasn't listening. He was staring across the station concourse. He took several seconds to answer.

'He's here.'

'What?' Charlotte asked.

'They're here,' Danny said. 'Don't look. Wire and his friend. Behind you.'

Danny noticed that Charlotte didn't glance over. She just carried on looking at him. That was good. He looked again, over her shoulder. Wire and Graham were at the far end of the station concourse, staring at Danny and Charlotte.

He could see they were talking. Graham pointed. In their direction.

'What are they doing?' Charlotte asked.

'I don't know. They might just be here for something else. It doesn't mean they're following us.'

'It's a bit of a coincidence,' Charlotte said, as

a loud announcement about trains came over the speakers.

'What?'

'It's a bit of a –'

'Stand up,' Danny said. 'They're coming. Don't look round. And go into WHSmith.'

Charlotte did exactly what he said. They turned their backs on the two men and went into the shop. As they did so Danny glanced back. They were fifty metres away now. Heading for the shop.

Now Charlotte looked back and she saw them.

'What do we do, Danny?'

Danny could hear fear in Charlotte's voice. For some reason it made him feel stronger.

'They can't touch us in here. There are hundreds of people around. Just look at the magazines. Stay near the till, where the staff can see us.'

Danny saw Charlotte was pale. Like she was really scared.

'If this isn't a coincidence all they're doing is checking us out. They don't know we know anything. All they saw was you in the toilet. Just act normal.'

They both picked up a magazine. And pretended to read.

Danny counted out a minute, then looked round again.

No one.

He glanced at Charlotte who was looking studiously at a magazine. About kittens.

Danny looked at his magazine. He was reading the same one.

They were both standing still, looking weird, reading the same magazine about kittens.

Danny wanted to laugh. But he'd seen something else. A pair of eyes. Paul Wire's eyes. Looking at him over the top of the magazine stands.

When their eyes met there was no change of expression from Wire. No frown or smile. No threat. Just a vacant look less than three metres away.

That felt to Danny more frightening than a threat would have. Normally if you caught a stranger's eye they smiled at you or looked away quickly. But Wire was still looking blankly at him.

Danny looked back at his kittens. At an article that was something to do with stopping kittens pooing in the house. But he couldn't take the words in.

Then he felt Charlotte leaning into him.

He glanced up at her.

'They're going,' she said.

Danny looked up. It was true. Wire and his friend were walking slowly out of the shop, on to the station concourse.

Neither Danny nor Charlotte felt like moving, even though the two men were leaving. They still had their kitten magazines open.

'Do you think that was a coincidence?' Charlotte asked.

Danny said nothing for a moment, thinking. 'No,' he said eventually. 'I don't.'

'That's not good, is it?' Charlotte said.

Danny shook his head. 'No. It isn't.'

BINMAN

The bus stopped and started, matching the sluggish speed of the city-centre traffic for the first twenty minutes. But, after they left the centre, it picked up its pace and moved smoothly past the giant park on the outskirts of the city.

Danny sat on the bus, frowning. Now Charlotte had gone home, he was alone and had time to think.

He wasn't sure what had gone on that morning with Paul Wire. Had he really followed Danny and Charlotte? A former City player? One whose name Danny used to chant at matches with his dad.

Why had he been in the Ladies in that pub?

Was he really involved with drugs?

And the biggest question: was Wire involved

in these burglaries like Anton thought? Or was he nothing to do with it?

And if he wasn't, Danny had no leads at all.

Danny looked around him. There were several younger people on the bus. On their way back from college, Danny supposed. Some were carrying files. Some were talking about being in the common room. They were seventeen or eighteen. About Emily's age.

The bus had to wait a few minutes to break out across the ring road. Then it accelerated out into the countryside.

Towards Alex Finn's house.

Where Danny had a little more investigating to do.

After he got off the bus, Danny waited on the far side of the road to Alex Finn's house. He was next to a country pub with benches, so he made sure he looked like he was with some of the drinkers sitting out enjoying the early-evening sun. He could easily be one of their children. And anyway, the TV crews hanging around, reporting on the attempted burglary, seemed to take up everyone's attention.

From here Danny could see a lot.

The driveway of Finn's house was cordoned off. A pair of officers were sifting through the gravel, centimetre by centimetre. A fingerprints person was dusting the doorway. Another was upstairs, visible through the window.

Finn's place was really nice. It looked like a farmhouse with an attached barn. There was a pair of fancy gates just off the road. Black-painted metal. And either side of the house, along a driveway, there were medium-sized trees.

As he watched the mêlée, Danny saw one of the people from the press pack leave the group and slip down the side of the house.

Danny could see it was a man with dark hair. But that was all.

What was he up to?

Danny had wanted to spend the whole time just watching the house, seeing what he could pick up. Following one individual meant he might miss things. But this was too tempting. Something unusual was about to happen. He was sure of it.

Danny moved from the pub and crossed the road. He needed to get closer. And no one was watching him. He was just a boy. Just a fan. That's what he would say if he was challenged.

The man with dark hair appeared to be moving down the side of the house. Slowly. Like Danny imagined a burglar would. In dark clothes too, so he wouldn't stand out, or catch anybody's eye.

Danny found a public footpath on the house side of the road and made his way down it, sweeping overhanging branches out of the way. This would get him close to the house. To see what this character was doing. To see if he could pick up any clues at all as to who had broken into Alex Finn's home.

Danny squatted and peered through the bushes.

And there he was. Going through the bins at the side of the house.

Danny was spellbound. The man was taking rubbish out of a wheelie bin he had turned on its side. Lifting pieces of paper out of lumps of food and fruit skins. Putting them in another bin bag.

Danny wondered first if he was a policeman, gathering evidence. But if he was he would be wearing some sort of uniform or overalls, like the others.

Danny decided to watch, regardless. This was

not normal behaviour. So it had to mean something. It might have nothing to do with the burglaries, but he might learn something anyway.

It was possible it did have something to do with the burglaries. Perhaps this was the burglar coming back, having hidden something, money perhaps, in the bins. Perhaps he was using the attention of the media on the front of the house to do what he needed to do.

The man went through everything in the bin, his back to Danny. If it was paper it went into his fresh bin bag. Otherwise it went back into the bin.

Danny kept on watching until the man stopped, sealed the bin bag, righted the wheelie bin and turned round.

Now Danny could see his face.

And that was what shocked him the most. The man's face.

It was Anton Holt.

SATURDAY

SATURDAY

HOW TO FOLLOW A SUSPECT

Danny had hardly slept since yesterday's events, he was so obsessed with cracking this crime.

The first thing he did, once he'd got to the café for another surveillance session, was text Holt. He had been wondering how to approach it: seeing Holt in the bins yesterday. He decided to be as straight as he could.

> **Saw you at the house yesterday.**
> **What were you up to?**
> **Danny**

He knew Holt would either text back instantly – or take hours.

This time it was instant.

Not me, Danny. Call you later.
AH

What did that mean? Danny wondered. That was crazy. It was clearly Holt. Danny had seen him with his own eyes.

So why was he denying it?

Perhaps because he couldn't text or email the truth, thinking someone other than Danny might read it?

Danny shook his head. Holt had been funny recently. And this whole going through Finn's bins and then lying about it was making things worse.

Danny sat and drank his tea. He needed to calm down and think. About everything. About what on earth he was involved in. This week. This year. The whole thing.

He was glad of one thing: that there was a different team of assistants in the café that morning. This was his third day here on the trot. They might start to wonder about him.

In fact, he was starting to wonder about the sense in coming here every day of the holidays himself. He thought about all the crime novels he'd read to his dad. He couldn't think of any that had the detective character going to the same café day after day, watching for one person who may or may not arrive. Crime novels were full of chases and excitement. Not just watching. But Danny also knew that in real life detectives sat and watched. For hours. For days. For weeks. He had read in the newspapers about operations to watch suspected terrorists. They watched them for months, gathering evidence, putting a case together. And quite often it came to nothing.

And if nothing happened here that was OK too. Danny had a lot to think about. A million questions about the burglars, about Wire and about the security guard. And now – although he couldn't believe he was thinking this – he had questions about Holt.

He took out his notebook and made a page out for each suspect.

Suspect one: Paul Wire.

Why was he a suspect?

Because Anton had had a tip from a solid source. Because he was obviously involved in very dodgy activities, such as hiding things in toilets. Because he followed Danny and Charlotte yesterday.

So he was dodgy. Clearly. And it meant he was

capable of burglary. But it didn't mean he was doing it.

Suspect two: the security guard.

Because the police had been reported to have arrested a security guard the night Danny was in the woods. Possibly the one who had chased him on the night of the François burglary. It was vague, but he was still a suspect.

Suspect three. Danny couldn't believe he was putting this down in his notebook. But he did. *Suspect three: Anton Holt.*

Why?

Because Danny had seen him at the scene of a crime and he couldn't explain it. That on its own would not have been enough. But Anton was being weird. And he'd denied being at the house the day before.

Danny didn't believe he was a suspect at all. He just couldn't afford to rule him out.

Suspect four: someone else.

Why?

Because, however much he liked to think one of his suspects was the burglar, Danny was not convinced. Not by a long way. And the most important thing was that he had to keep an open mind.

Danny drank his cup of tea slowly. He was getting a bit sick of tea. He wished he'd ordered a Coke.

And then he saw Wire standing at the door of the pub. Just like that. He'd not even seen him arrive. But there he was, smoking a cigarette. 10.55 a.m. Danny put it in his notebook.

10.55   Wire arrives at Precinct pub. Smokes cigarette.

11.00   Pub opens.

11.03   Two men enter pub. Wire. And Francis Graham.

11.35   Wire leaves pub. Heading towards railway station.

Danny was on his feet. Now he was going to get to do the following, as opposed to being followed. As he made his way out of the café, a voice in his head was telling him not to. Based on the scare he'd had from Wire yesterday. But what could he do? This was his best lead. This was the chance to get to grips with a series of football crimes that showed no signs of ending.

He remembered how he'd followed people

before. Notably another footballer, Matt McGee, in Moscow, six months earlier, when he'd been investigating a Russian billionaire who was intent on murdering England keepers. He had tried to use techniques he'd learned in a book on being a spy:

- Follow at a distance
- Try to be on the other side of the road, not directly in your target's footsteps
- If your target looks round, keep going, don't stop or try to hide, behave normally
- Act like you are going somewhere, not following

In Russia he had ended up trailing the player down a long busy road, then going down by the river. Making it obvious Danny was following the player.

Today Danny wouldn't have the same problem.

Because it was difficult for Wire to notice he was being followed. Every ten metres or so someone greeted him. He was an ex-City player, he was famous. They were out in the centre of town. Danny saw that Wire kept his head down, trying not to be spotted. But, when he was, he'd just give a quick wave or nod.

Danny followed seventy metres behind. Through the Saturday morning shoppers: people with bags bulging, groups of girls his age. He stayed at the same distance behind Wire until they reached the railway station. And another pub.

This man seems to spend his life in pubs.

The pub had two entrances. One was a huge glass front that had been rolled back so that the pub spilled out on to the station concourse. And there – right in the middle of the entrance – was a massive TV screen. Showing Spurs v. City. About to kick off.

The concourse was large. There were shops and cafés either side. A glass roof let light in high above. And the sound of footsteps filled the chamber.

Danny stood in a small group of younger people and passers-by who were watching the game without getting a drink. It was ideal. He could watch Wire in the pub from the cover of this crowd. *And* see the match. Perfection. He bought a Coke from the shop at the end of the station concourse and watched.

The first thing he noticed was Wire being

bought a lot of drinks. Other customers kept bringing him bottles. Becks beer, Danny noted. And, even though the game had started, people were desperate to talk to him.

The match was a good one too. Meaningful. City in fifth place in the Premier League. Spurs fourth. Whoever won would be in a Champions League spot. It was a key game.

The first half was tight. Both teams playing deep, not taking risks. A lot of the drinkers were talking, messing about, not looking at the match at all.

At half-time a surge of men headed for the bar and the toilets. Including Wire.

Danny wasn't quite sure what to do. He could follow, get into the pub, see what Wire was up to. But then he might blow his cover. Or he could stay here, assume that Wire would come back to his place. Then he noticed Wire had taken off his jacket and thrown it over a chair.

That meant he was staying. Leaving his jacket. Keeping a chair. And several full bottles of lager.

Danny was right: before long Wire had returned and was drinking again.

The second half of the game was better than the first. Both teams were attacking more. And City had brought on a substitute. It had opened up. Ten minutes into the second half City broke away. Danny joined in the shouts. It was three against two, City's forwards streaming onwards up the pitch. Danny noticed City's new striker, Robert Jones, move wide of his marker, just as the midfielder, Lucas Craxford, passed the ball to him.

Now he was in space, on the edge of the box. He controlled the ball with his first touch, waited for the keeper, Mark Bull, to come off his line, then he clipped it over him.

1–0.

City were winning.

Danny jumped up and down, catching the eyes of the people he'd been standing with.

Grinning.

He loved it when City scored. It was even better while he was carrying out surveillance.

Brilliant.

He looked to see how Wire was celebrating. But realized, to his horror, that he couldn't spot him.

Where was he?

Danny looked to see if Wire's jacket was still slung over the chair. But that was gone too.

Paul Wire had disappeared. And Danny had to think fast.

FOLLOW THAT CAB

Where had Paul Wire gone? He was nowhere to be seen.

Had he gone for a train?

Caught a taxi? Headed back to the Precinct?

Danny had to choose. Use his intuition.

If Wire had taken a train there was no way Danny would find him in the hundreds of people walking in and out of shopping arcades and from the station.

If he'd gone for a taxi or to the other pub he'd have turned left and out into City Square. That meant that it was a two in three chance he'd gone that way. It was Danny's best bet: the most likely explanation. So he ran. Out of the station. Into the city.

He looked across City Square towards the Precinct pub. He saw the backs of a hundred heads. Half of them could have been Wire. He looked back at the taxi queue. There was no one there. No taxis.

Danny stamped his foot. He'd lost Wire.

He swore under his breath. Wire was his only decent lead and it was nearly the end of the school holidays. When school was back on Danny would have far less time to do stuff like this.

Maybe he'd just lost his best chance of solving this crime.

He stared out across City Square until his view was broken by a car. A taxi. And in the taxi, talking heatedly into a mobile phone, was Paul Wire. Wearing his hoody jacket, half-hiding his face.

How had that happened?

Danny looked back at the taxi rank. A second taxi had just arrived. He made a quick decision. He'd get a cab too. He'd taken out money to do Holt's surveillance, so he could afford it. He looked for Wire's taxi. It was stuck in traffic around City Square. Still catchable.

Danny ran to the second taxi and jumped in. He'd read several books where detectives had jumped into cabs in New York – or somewhere like that – and had said, 'Follow that cab!' It was something he'd always dreamed of doing.

'Where to, son?' the taxi driver said. She was a middle-aged woman with short blonde hair.

'Follow that cab!' Danny said, grinning.

'You a joker?' she said, smiling.

'No. Please. Follow it. Will you?'

The woman smiled. 'It's not dangerous, is it?'

'No,' Danny said. 'Course not.'

The taxi ride was not a breakneck chase of squealing tyres and minor collisions. It was carried out at a maximum of 15 miles an hour, stop-start through the congested city centre. Danny wondered if he would have been better to walk.

But then the traffic left the centre and headed north. Past rows and rows of terraced houses. Towards the city park, the way he'd come the day before on the bus.

It had started to rain.

After a few minutes Wire's taxi took a left and headed along the side of some playing fields – football and rugby posts casting shadows across muddy grass. The fields were known as Soldiers' Fields. Danny's dad had told him that during the

First World War, the army had trained soldiers here. This was only a mile or so from the City FC training facility. Right where Danny had to be later to watch Kofi play.

His taxi followed Wire's.

'Shall I stay back a bit, love?' the driver asked.

'Yes please,' Danny said.

And it was good they did, because Wire's taxi stopped suddenly, out in the open, hundreds of metres from any buildings. Danny saw Wire climbing out, his hoody still up.

He wondered what to do next. *Drive past*, he thought. *Go on, then double back, so Wire doesn't sense he's being followed.*

'What now?'

'Can you go past them, please?' Danny said. 'Then stop around the corner?'

'You're the boss,' the taxi driver said.

Danny turned his head away from Wire as they passed. In case he recognized him from the day before.

A few seconds later his taxi turned a corner and stopped. Danny paid and got out.

'Be careful, love,' the driver said, handing him a blank receipt.

'I will, thanks.'

And then she was gone.

Danny looked back at the fields in the light rain. There was Wire, walking across a football pitch. Danny followed by walking along the path that led around Soldiers' Fields. He would have to walk quickly. But he was only 300 metres from Wire. Not too far. Not too near.

Wire seemed to be heading towards some houses on the far side of the fields. The houses here were posh. Seriously posh. Danny estimated they'd have at least six bedrooms. They were all detached and made of old stone.

When Wire reached the first house he picked up his speed, cutting up a road. Danny had to jog to keep the former player in his sights.

But he had to be careful. Wire was glancing around all the time, seeing who was near him.

Danny followed Wire down two streets of the big houses. He wondered where he was going. To another pub? To a friend's house? Home? Did Wire live round here? Danny tried to keep his mind open. He didn't want to assume anything.

And then Wire disappeared into a hedge. At least that's what it looked like.

Danny picked up his speed and – remembering

one of his surveillance tricks – crossed to the other side of the road. There was a chance Wire had spotted him, and was hiding in the hedge, ready to jump out at him.

As Danny passed the spot where Wire had disappeared, he glanced nervously to his right.

Allotments. He had gone into some allotments, a grid of small gardens for local people to grow vegetables.

Except he wasn't there. No one was. Danny was stumped again.

And then he saw Wire, pulling at a fence at the far end of the allotments.

Danny found a place to hide and watched.

Wire struggled at first, the fence too strong to get through. Finally, he managed to prise a piece of the wood outwards to allow him to slip in between two fence posts and into a garden.

So whose house is that? Danny thought. Another footballer's? And how did Wire know it was empty? Maybe he'd been told. City were still playing at Spurs. If it was a City player's house, then he would be away. But would his family?

These thoughts ran through Danny's mind as

he walked around the edges of the allotments, pleased there was no one there to watch him.

He soon found the gap that Wire had made in the fence. He peeped through. There was a long garden, very overgrown, not looked after at all – it didn't seem like the garden of a footballer. But the back door of the house was wide open, the lock smashed.

Wire had to be inside.

This was proof: Wire *was* the burglar.

So now what?

What would a detective from one of Danny's dad's books do?

Follow him into the house?

Call the police, to get them to arrest him?

Just watch?

Film some evidence?

Danny was confused. Again. He wished he could be more decisive.

But then his decision was made for him.

Two men had arrived at the allotments.

Gardeners.

Danny slipped into the garden of the house, allowing the fence to close behind him. Now he was trespassing, like Wire. He looked up at the window of the big house. The paint on the window frames was peeling. The satellite dish was hanging loose on the chimney. And the state of the house set his mind thinking. Why was it so unkempt? Clearly no one was using the garden. It could mean something.

Then Danny was distracted by a figure at one of the windows. Wire. Danny could see him from behind as he searched the house. And there was Danny standing in the garden. All Wire had to do was look round and he'd see him.

Danny couldn't go back into the allotments. And there was no way around the side of the house. So, to avoid being seen by Wire and with no other thought about what to do in his head, he rushed towards the house.

He went inside.

What was he going to do now?

TRAPPED

Danny entered the house through the kitchen. And it was a *big* kitchen. It had a large table in the centre and a giant cappuccino-making machine by the cooker. It was also spectacularly clean.

This was a strange house. Some signs that the house was abandoned. Other signs that someone lived here.

Once in, Danny stood still and listened. He needed to gather information. The first thing was always to listen. He had learned that. There were footsteps upstairs in the room above. Paul Wire searching the house.

The second thing Danny did was ask himself what *he* was doing in this house. At first it had been to avoid Wire seeing him. Was that all he wanted? Just to be safe, then leave? Or did he want more? Could he get proof that Paul Wire was behind the footballers' burglaries?

And could he do it without getting caught?

Danny took out his mobile phone and set it to video. Then he went to the front door of the house to make sure it was open as well as the back. He'd read about this trick in his book about burglaries. Have more than one escape route prepared.

Now all he had to do was get one piece of footage of Wire in this house, then he could go.

Easy?

He doubted it. But if he could do it he would have solved and proved one of the great football crimes of all time. It was too much to resist.

Danny walked into the hall and looked up the staircase. It was wide and curved round as it reached the next floor.

If he could just get a couple of seconds of video of Wire in the house . . .

Danny moved slowly up the stairs. He could hear Wire going through one of the rooms, pulling drawers open, dropping stuff on the floor. When he got to the top of the staircase Danny saw a reflection of Wire in a mirror of the bedroom, his back to the door. He seemed to be putting something on the floor in the doorway. Some sort of file or folder.

Danny raised his phone and pressed record.

He looked at his screen. There was Paul Wire, on his tiptoes, pulling boxes down from the top of a cupboard, throwing them behind himself on to a bed. And there he was going through the contents of the boxes.

This was good.

Every few seconds Danny glanced down the staircase. He had to keep it in his mind that Wire was not his only threat. The other threat was the unlikely – but possible – chance that another person might come up the stairs. The police? A security guard? The owners?

Just a few seconds more, he told himself. Then out.

He needed a better shot of Wire's face. That was his only problem. He had to get closer.

That made it more of a risk.

But he was here now, wasn't he?

Danny walked slowly towards the room Wire was ransacking. He could see the player still had his back to the door, going through a heap of things on the bed.

Danny moved to the other side of the door. If

Wire came out now he would cut off Danny's escape route. But it would be OK. Danny had surprise on his side.

He knelt and pointed the camera at Wire, so he could catch him at the moment he turned round. Danny was in the position of a sprinter at the beginning of a race. He'd get his image, then he'd be off.

Wire had yet to turn round. But Danny kept filming.

Until his attention was caught by the file that Wire had put by the door.

Why had Wire put that by the door? So he could take it when he left? Because it was one of the things he was looking for?

Maybe.

If Danny could just see what it was he was taking. What could it be? Papers, perhaps? What papers could be so interesting a burglar would take them? Deeds to the house? Details of bank accounts?

And then he saw Wire take out his mobile phone. Wire moved further into the room, so Danny couldn't see him. But he could still hear him.

'I've got the file,' Wire said.

Danny glanced at the file. He moved a bit closer.

'Yeah. Just seeing if there's anything else. You know. Something interesting.'

Another pause. Danny had his hand inches from the file.

'OK. I'll be out of here in one minute,' Wire concluded.

Danny listened to Wire going through some drawers or a cupboard. He reached out. He had to know. He kept his left hand steady against the door, filming, and leaned to reach the papers with his right.

Danny wasn't sure what happened first.

Whether he fell and then Wire looked round. Or whether Wire looked round and then he fell.

Either way, it was bad. Very bad.

'Who the hell are you?' Wire shouted, stepping backwards in shock.

Danny didn't reply. He scrambled to his feet to run, grabbing the file first.

But the problem was that – in his confusion and fear – he ran the wrong way. He ran into the *back* of the house. Away from the stairs.

'Get here, you . . .' Wire shouted.

And Wire was behind him.

Danny dashed along a corridor, gripping the file in his right hand. More stairs at the end. Although the house had seemed big, now the corridors felt narrow and small. He was trapped with no way out. Going up was mad, but he couldn't go down.

So he went up.

To the attic.

The sound of his footsteps hammering on the stairs.

He expected to hear Wire's feet behind him.

But when he got to the top there was silence. So he looked down. And there was Paul Wire looking *up* at him. Smiling.

'You're the lad from the pub,' Wire said, not asking a question.

Danny said nothing.

'Is there a helicopter up there? An escape ladder?'

Wire's voice was horribly calm. That scared Danny even more than he was scared already. Wire sounded so comfortable.

Danny looked at the two doors at the top of the stairs. One was an ordinary painted wooden door. The other seemed to be reinforced. It had bars across it, although it was open.

'I've got you trapped,' Wire said, smiling again, 'and now I'm coming to get you. *Burglar in fall as he breaks into house*. That sounds like a good headline.'

Danny swallowed.

Paul Wire put his foot on the bottom step.

This was it, Danny thought. His worst scrape yet. And he had absolutely no way out of it.

Paul Wire was thundering up the stairs.

PANIC ROOM

Danny leapt backwards and almost fell into one of the rooms at the top of the stairs, tripping on a step. Without thinking it through, he went into the room with the reinforced door and swung it behind him.

But the door was heavy. Much heavier than Danny had expected. It hadn't slammed shut as he'd wanted. In fact, it was still open. And Danny could hear that Paul Wire was nearing the top of the stairs.

Wire would be able to get in.

Danny flung himself at the heavy door, his shoulder hitting it hard.

Wire made it to the top of the stairs just as Danny hit it. Wire's hands had been on the door as Danny pushed. Danny heard him cry out as he fell backwards. Then he heard a strange noise. An electric whirr.

What was that?

He looked up at the door. And was surprised to see that it was solid metal on the inside.

Then he heard Wire banging, trying to get in. But it was obvious to Danny that the door was locked. The noise had been the door locking itself automatically. And there was a sign by the door, an illuminated image of a padlock. Red.

Danny managed a half smile. He was safe. For now.

He stood to take in the rest of the room. It was not what he had expected to see in the top room of a house like this. He had imagined a bedroom or an office. Not this.

The most striking thing in the room was the huge plasma screen on the chimney breast. It was as big as the TV screen in Didier François' house. Or bigger. But this one was a split screen, showing sixteen views from security cameras of the house Danny was in. Top left showed Paul Wire banging on the door. His door.

Danny watched, fascinated. He could see Wire on the screen ahead of him, at the same time as he could hear him for real banging on the door behind him. It felt weird.

After a few seconds Danny watched Wire head down the stairs. The top left camera tracked him as he went down. Then Danny noticed movement on another part of the screen. Wire was on the first-floor landing now. On another screen. At the point where he had left the file.

And that was where he was looking now. Danny watched him scanning the landing, then looking down into the hallway below. Then he saw Wire sprint back up the stairs as he realized Danny had the file.

The banging on the door was harder now. Danny could hear Wire shouting '. . . the papers . . . the . . . papers.' Then a stream of swear words.

Danny glanced at the file he'd picked up. The one Wire had wanted. It was on the floor near the door. He must have dropped it there as he came in. What the hell was in there that was making Wire go so berserk?

Wire was kicking at the wall around the door. And Danny feared it would cave in. Then he'd be helpless.

Danny looked around the room. He didn't

know what he was after, but he needed something that would help him. If Wire got in, he'd really hurt Danny.

Next to the padlock sign by the door there was a second illuminated sign that he'd not noticed before. It bore two words: POLICE EMERGENCY.

Without thinking of the consequences, overwhelmed by fear, Danny hit it.

For a moment everything went quiet. Wire had stopped attacking the door and wall. And Danny could hear a voice coming from a speaker saying something outside in the stairway. Some sort of warning. He thought it must be a pre-recorded warning being played to Wire. To say the police were coming.

And Danny realized that if the police *were* coming for Wire, then they were coming for him too.

So why did Wire continue to just stand there? Danny watched him on the screen. It was like he was paralysed.

Danny used the time to check the rest of the room. Apart from what looked like a control panel and a computer screen, it was like a small sitting room. The sofa looked like it would convert into a bed. And in the corner there was a fridge next to a door.

Danny found himself caught as to what to do. He was locked in a strange room in a house he was trespassing in. A violent man wanted to get in. The police were on the way.

Behind the door there was a toilet, a sink and a shower.

It's a panic room, Danny thought. A room you could hide in if a burglar or kidnapper came into your house. Danny wondered if the people who built it had ever thought it would be protecting a fourteen-year-old boy from an ex-professional footballer.

Then Danny caught sight of one of the screens. Trained on the outside of the house, the front garden. The path.

They were here already – the police.

Two white marked cars. Four uniformed officers in black. All heading up the garden path.

Danny watched Wire suddenly come to his senses. Something must have told him the police were here. Snapped him out of his trance – or whatever it was he had been doing. Then he saw Wire thundering down the stairs. Flitting from camera to camera as he sprinted through the house. Running across a landing, then down another staircase.

He's heading for the back door, Danny thought, as he saw the police coming through the front.

As they did, Wire hit the bottom of the stairs.

Danny watched from a camera placed above him. Watched Wire freeze on the spot as he looked to his right. And that was when Danny saw him on another camera as well. The same camera that showed the police. A second later two of the police officers were chasing Wire to the left.

Now they were in the kitchen. The room through which Danny had entered the house. Danny watched the three people come together, a heap of bodies, a kitchen table.

And, eventually, all five people were together on the same screen. Two police holding Wire, one on each arm. The other two opening the front door, leading the way out.

Maybe, Danny thought, *I am going to get out of this. Maybe they think Wire is here on his own. They might just go.*

But then Danny felt as if a cold hand had gripped itself round his heart. Because he could see – in the screen showing the front garden – that, as he still struggled, Paul Wire was pointing. Pointing back at the house. And he knew that the footballer was telling them about him.

THE LOFT

Danny knew that he couldn't hang around. And that he certainly couldn't stay in the panic room. If the police found him here, how was he going to explain himself? He was one strike away from having a police record and all the consequences that brought. Trouble at home. No chance of a job in the police. That sort of thing.

But how was he going to get away?

The police were already in the hallway of the house, about to come up the stairs. He had just seconds.

Danny slammed his hand on to the illuminated red pad by the door, grabbing the file. The door opened immediately.

He turned to head down the stairs. But two steps down he heard voices.

'Police!'

Danny jumped back up the stairs.

Where now? Back into the panic room?

If he went in there the police would either get in or sit there and wait for him to come out. Wire had no doubt told them he was in there.

And then Danny had an idea. The start of a plan.

If Wire had told them he was in the panic room, then maybe he could buy himself some time. Danny pulled the panic-room door shut as hard as he could.

He listened.

And there it was: that strange electrical noise. The panic room had locked itself.

Then Danny lunged into the other doorway, expecting the police to be coming up the staircase at any point.

He pushed the door to, then quietly slid the small bolt across to lock the door.

Now what?

He could hear the police on the stairs. Two voices. He put his head to the door.

'Is there anyone in there?' one of them shouted.

'Hello?' Another shout. A woman's voice.

'Do you think there is?' the man said, quieter now.

'Maybe. But I'm not sure I buy it. A teenager following him around the house? Unlikely. But we have to take it seriously.'

Danny had his back to the door as he listened. He was looking for a way out. The attic room was set up as a spare bedroom. He glanced through the window. There was no way out there. Unless he fancied climbing on to the roof.

He looked for another way. The fireplace? Could he climb up the chimney? Danny told himself not to be so stupid. The hole was tiny.

He had to face it. He was trapped. He would go out there and tell them the truth. If they didn't believe him, then at least *he* knew he was doing things for the right reasons.

Danny stood up straight and gripped the door handle.

This was it.

The end.

Except it wasn't. Because Danny had noticed something. A hole in the ceiling. A way into the roof. A loft. The ceiling here was low. Very low. And his mind went back to Paul Wire in the toilets of that pub. Hide where no one would look.

Danny took a stool from next to the bed. He

set it under the hole in the ceiling, stood on it and eased the ceiling panel out of the way, passing the file up into the space above him. He was about to lift himself up when he heard the door handle of his room go again. Someone was twisting it one way, then the other.

'This one's locked too,' the policeman said.

'Really?' replied the policewoman.

'Yeah.'

'Force it.'

And, with that, there was a smash and the door flew open, bouncing off the wall and ricocheting back at the two police officers who were staring into the room.

The empty room.

The two police officers shrugged and turned their attention back to the panic-room door. But above the room they saw as empty, in the loft, his hands and feet lodged on the beams that were holding the ceiling up, the file next to him, Danny Harte was poised, too terrified to move.

Half an hour later, Danny was still in the roof. He had found himself a more comfortable position. His arms and legs along the beams, so it was almost as if he was lying down. But things were beginning to hurt.

After a lot of long silences and shifting of feet, the police radioed back to their HQ and asked for some sort of code. Once they had it they keyed it in and opened the panic room.

'Empty,' said the policewoman.

The policeman said nothing. Although Danny thought he heard him tut. This was important. Danny needed them to leave so he could get away. But would they? Or would they stay? Or, worse, search the house properly?

The policewoman was on the radio again. 'Nothing here. The house is empty.'

Then a silence.

'He might say that,' she replied down the radio, 'but there's no one here.'

Then she went quiet again. Listening, Danny judged.

'OK,' she said finally. 'We're coming back.'

And Danny breathed out. They were going. What a relief. And he turned his attention to the papers in the file.

KOFI'S GAME

Danny walked through the woods to the City training ground, avoiding the roads and any chance of being seen. He lifted his feet over exposed roots, ducking beneath great trails of ivy that came down from the trees and wondered if he was becoming paranoid, thinking that people would be looking for him. He'd been so freaked out by being trapped in the house with Wire that he knew he was bound to be feeling extra sensitive.

He had read some of the contents of the file. Papers about City FC, meaning Wire had known what he was looking for. Even if there didn't seem to be anyone living there right now, perhaps this house was something to do with the football club. Most of the papers had been legal documents that he had struggled to make sense of.

Especially in an unlit loft space. But one sheet had struck him as particularly strange. A letter on headed paper – Forza FC headed paper. Written in Italian.

What had that been about? What could City possibly have to do with Forza FC?

Perhaps he shouldn't have hidden the papers in the loft. His thinking had been that he should not leave the house with them. That would have made him a burglar. So he had left them.

Now he was starting to wish he'd taken the risk. He needed to talk to someone. To help him arrange his thoughts.

He called Charlotte.

'Hey Danny.'

'Hi. Do you want to go and watch Kofi play this afternoon?'

'Yeah, OK, that would be good.'

'I'm going there now,' Danny said. 'It starts in an hour or so.'

'I'll see you there.'

Danny loved the uncomplicated way Charlotte would just do things. Lots of other people had to make things difficult and try to change simple plans. But Charlotte seemed to be free of all that.

*

The City FC training facility was buzzing when Danny got there.

Coming along in a car you wouldn't think there was anything much there. It was just a long road bordered by trees and overgrown patches of land. And if you were driving quickly you could miss the small sign:

CITY FC TRAINING FACILITY AND ACADEMY

Danny came to the academy from the woods at the other side of the road. A large coach arrived and turned as he emerged. He noticed the logo on the front. Manchester United. It was the Man U under-eighteens squad arriving for the game. Some of the best under-eighteen footballers in the world. Danny smiled. He would love to see City beat this lot. And he was looking forward to seeing Kofi play too.

He brushed himself down, aware that he would look strange turning up with leaves and twigs in his hair and on his clothes.

The academy looked amazing. Danny could see the distinctive wood and glass front from the road now. He had never been here before, but he'd seen pictures of it on the club website.

He walked through the gates, following in the wake of the Man U coach.

To his right there was a car park and the wood-fronted building, to his left indoor pitches inside steel-framed buildings that looked like a posh sports centre to Danny. Danny looked again to his right to see a large number of people stood around in the foyer. And, as he stared, one of them emerged from the group, a young man with dark hair and a black jacket, making his way to Danny.

Holt. Anton Holt. And he was smiling.

'Danny. It's good to see you.' Holt looked smart, freshly shaved, which wasn't always the case.

They shook hands. Danny and Holt always shook hands. Danny took it as a sign that Holt respected him, didn't treat him like a child. And a sign that things were OK between them. That Holt still trusted him.

'Have you heard?' Holt asked.

'About Wire?'

'Yeah.' Holt paused, narrowing his eyes. 'It was you, wasn't it?' he said. 'You're the teenager the police were looking for.'

Danny nodded. 'I was there,' he admitted. But

he knew this was as far as his confession would go. Holt was his friend above all: they had been through too much together. He felt bad for having him down as a suspect but he knew Holt wouldn't have judged him for this even if he knew.

Then Holt held his hand up to stop Danny. Other journalists were nearby now. They might overhear.

'So what do you know?' Danny asked Holt.

'Wire was arrested outside a house about two miles from here. He was breaking in. Some sort of alarm went off. They got him easily. And, apparently, he confessed to being the football burglar. Some people on the street overheard him.'

'So he claimed it's him?' Danny asked.

'Yeah,' Holt said. 'It's all finished. He'll confess. He'll plead guilty. End of story.'

Danny nodded. He didn't want to say anything, but he wasn't 100% sure of the story. It was too easy. But there were too many other people about to raise his doubts with Holt. And he wasn't sure it was the right time.

'But there's more,' another voice said.

'This is Sam,' Anton said to Danny, gesturing

to a tall blond man with a cheesy smile. 'He writes for *footballgossip.com*.'

'Hi,' Sam said, looking closely at Danny.

'Hello.'

'More . . . what?' Holt said. 'The boy?'

'Yes,' Sam said. 'Wire has claimed there was a teenager in the house. About your age, son. And some other people who live round there say they saw him too.'

'What? He was Wire's accomplice?' Danny asked, trying to deflect the idea that he was the same age as the spotted boy. Sam obviously hadn't heard Danny confess to Holt.

'No,' Sam answered. 'No. It's not clear. But Wire denied that. Apparently he said he was responsible for the burglaries alone.'

'How do you know that?' Danny asked, still trying to sound like he was an innocent boy and not someone with a lot more invested in finding out more. Still aware that Sam was looking at him closely. Thinking that this other journalist recognized Danny from the photo fit. And it all came back to him. Before the house. Before the panic room. The fact that a photo fit of a boy looking just like Danny was plastered all over the city. Danny wondered whether he should talk it through with Holt. Once he got him on his own.

'Secret sources,' Sam said, tapping his nose. Then his eyes skipped over Danny's head as he watched someone behind Danny.

Danny and Holt looked round.

Charlotte was walking towards them. She waved.

'Has it started?' she asked, brushing against Danny.

'Not yet,' Danny replied.

Charlotte saw Holt. 'Hi Anton. How are you?'

But just then Holt's phone went off. He glanced at the screen and held his hand up, merely nodding at Charlotte. Danny knew that meant this was private and watched the journalist walk away from them. Sam, the other journalist, had drifted away too.

'Was it something I said?' Charlotte joked.

'Probably,' Danny smiled. 'Listen, there's a bit of time to go before kick-off.' Danny pointed at the empty playing fields ahead of them. Several pitches, side by side, all perfectly groomed and green, pitches that would have looked great in a Premier League stadium. There was a small stall selling cups of tea and hot dogs. 'Shall we get a drink?'

'So run through it again,' Charlotte said, once Danny had detailed the morning's events. 'You were in the house when Wire got arrested?'

Danny nodded. As they'd had their drinks – Coke for Danny, water for Charlotte – he had told her about his morning.

'But he *didn't* see you?'

'No, he did. Before I found the panic room.'

'Did he recognize you?'

'Yes.'

'But you got away? And he got arrested.' Charlotte smiled. 'So it's all OK now.'

'Sort of,' Danny said. There were things in his mind that he'd not worked out.

Charlotte's smile faded. 'What?' she asked.

'I'm just not sure about Wire. I know Holt put us on to him. And I know he was there. But he wasn't in the house for money. He wanted those papers. And when he knew he couldn't have the papers, he went crazy. Crazy enough to stay and try to get me, which led to him getting caught. He could have escaped.' Danny was beginning to wish he hadn't left the files at the house – to wish he'd spent longer looking at them.

'So?'

'So he wasn't stealing money and valuables like the other robberies. It was like he was there for a different reason,' Danny said, pausing. 'And I've read about burglars. They don't change like that. It's almost as if Wire was two different kinds of burglar. Which is why I'm not sure he is the one who burgled the other houses.'

'Well I am,' Charlotte said, draining her bottle of water. 'Look, here come the players.'

BAG SNATCH

The burglar climbed out of his soft-top convertible. He felt good stepping out, standing, looking around. He hoped that someone would be looking at him, even though he was embarrassed about having a bandaged hand. It was a new car. He'd bought it with a large cash deposit, courtesy of Didier François, and put the rest on his credit card.

But no one was looking: the car park was empty. That meant the game would have started and he'd missed the beginning. But he wasn't bothered about that.

In fact, today, the little things were not bothering him at all. Because the thing that was bothering him was big. Very big. And that thing, or person, was Paul Wire. And to think he used to worship the man.

He had heard the news on the radio, then checked it out on the Internet. Paul Wire had been arrested burgling someone's house. And he'd confessed. To *all* the robberies. All of them! So now everyone thought Wire was the famous burglar.

Not him.

'Who does he think he is?' the burglar said, letting loose a string of swear-words.

A pair of women walking two dogs gave him a wide berth. He knew they'd heard him swearing to himself. Maybe they thought he was mad. But he didn't care what people thought. And maybe they were right: maybe he was mad. Maybe he was going to do something *extremely* mad.

He walked along a tarmac path that had a fence on each side, overgrowing woods beyond them. He was heading for the City FC training pitches to watch the youth team play.

The glory should be his. Not some washed-up, drug-dealing footballer. Why should Paul Wire get it all? Hadn't he already had enough? He carried on talking to himself about what he was going to do. How he was going to make sure that everyone knew that Wire was just an amateur.

On the City FC chat rooms that he hated, but read because he liked the way the fans thought they knew who was burgling footballers, they were saying it was gangsters.

Gangsters?

Idiots. They didn't even know what a gangster was.

He wanted everyone to know it was *him*. Not gangsters. Not Paul Wire.

On one of the chat rooms he had read a bit more. It had actually been very useful. A City fan had seen Wire being arrested. Apparently he had shouted to the police that there was someone else in the house. He'd been ranting and raving about some teenager who was in there too. Short dark hair. Fourteen or fifteen. The description sounded familiar. The burglar thought he had a good idea who that was.

It was obvious.

That was something else he was going to have to sort out.

He had reached the gates of the training complex now. As he walked through them, the security guard nodded to him.

'All right, Peter,' the burglar said. He knew the

security guard. Because he used to come here every day.

'Now then, Ian. Come to watch the lads?'

He nodded.

Once he was over the car park and on to the edge of the pitches, he stood at the side of the mobile canteen. It was put there to feed the families of the players, and other people who came to watch.

Who could he see?

The first thing he noticed was there were loads more journalists. He could see three or four he'd met before. He looked on to the pitch. He recognized a few players he knew there.

And then he saw him: Danny. So he *was* here.

And look who was with him: the girl. The nice one. What was her name? Charlotte. That was it. She'd been a bit of a tease when they'd met before. But he knew she liked him. It was the way she looked at him.

He smiled for the first time in hours. This was going to be an interesting afternoon.

But first he had a bit of business to attend to. There were still a few minutes to go before half-time.

Making sure everyone was watching the football, and not him, he backed behind the mobile canteen and headed towards the dressing rooms the footballers had come from.

They'd be empty now. All he needed was the code to the door. And he knew that well enough. 1-9-2-7. The year City FC had been formed. How stupid a code was that? People always chose something obvious. They were asking to be robbed.

Once the burglar was inside the complex he found the home dressing room. Benches round all four walls, hooks above the benches hung with jackets and bags. He patted each jacket to check for a wallet or some money. But there was nothing. No one would be stupid enough to leave money around. Even teenage footballers would not be naive enough to make such a mistake.

Then he looked at the bags on the benches. He immediately saw a bag that stood out. It was a deep green holdall. Mock leather. Cheap and nasty. Not the kind of bag any self-respecting footballer should have.

It was, of course, Kofi Danquah's bag. No question.

The man unzipped it quickly. He found hard

pitch boots, a towel, a phone, a watch, a wallet. A history book about the city they lived in. Other things, bits of paper.

He couldn't believe the wallet. He looked inside it. Lots of money. Cash. At least £200. So someone was stupid enough to leave a wallet here, after all! The young man zipped up the bag and lifted it off the bench.

That would do nicely.

Very nicely indeed, thought Ian Mills.

BLACKMAIL

Just before half-time Danny saw one of the City FC coaches speak to Kofi. Kofi had been warming up and Danny thought it was likely he'd be coming on after the break.

He saw the coach looking at the underside of Kofi's boots. Then Kofi pointed towards the large building behind Danny. The coach looked at his watch and gestured that Kofi should go.

'He's got the wrong boots,' Danny said to Charlotte.

'Is that bad?'

'It could be. They might not let him play,' Danny explained. 'If he's got his soft pitch boots on, for instance. They might have too long studs. He could injure himself, twist his ankle.'

They watched their friend run at half pace

towards what Danny assumed was the dressing room.

The burglar heard the footsteps coming quickly down the corridor. He sensed someone was coming towards him. Maybe he'd been spotted on a security camera. But he knew there was no point in panicking. If he was caught, he was caught. All he needed to do was to remain calm.

He moved into the shower area. He looked around for something to defend himself with. The shower fittings were the only things in the space that was otherwise just white tiles. A showerhead? he wondered. No, they were too light. Then he saw the metal rod that was used to hold the showerheads on the wall. He touched one. Steel. Heavy steel. That would do.

Before the footsteps came into the room, he swiftly ripped one off the wall.

It came off easily. It was heavy. Nice and heavy. You could easily knock a grown man out with this. Even kill one if you really wanted to.

Kofi dashed into the dressing room. He went straight to where he had hung his jacket.

His bag was gone.

'My bag?' he said to himself.

He spent a minute looking at every coat and bag, to be sure he had not missed his, or to see if his was under another. But it was useless.

It was not in the room. He had no choice but to go back to the coach and tell him. He did not have his hard pitch boots with him. It was likely he would not be able to play. This was his first chance in the under-eighteens. And he had blown it.

Kofi felt terrible.

And then he remembered sometimes the boys hid each other's bags for a joke. The showers. He'd not checked there.

Danny wondered where Kofi had got to. It was half-time now. Danny could see his coach looking towards the buildings, then at his watch. He could also see a police car, on the edge of the car park.

'Something's wrong,' he said to Charlotte, who was watching the players having their team talks.

'What?'

'Kofi should be back. And now the police are here.'

'He's coming,' Charlotte said. 'Look.'

And Danny saw Kofi running towards him. Faster now.

'My bag has gone,' Kofi said, slightly breathless, when he reached them.

'Where is it?' Danny asked, feeling stupid for saying something like that.

'I need my other boots,' Kofi went on.

'I'll help you,' Danny said.

'But they're not there.'

'We'll look again,' Danny insisted.

Kofi nodded and Danny joined him, jogging across the fields again, after Kofi had asked a team-mate to explain to the coach.

Almost as soon as Danny and Kofi had gone, Charlotte sensed someone behind her. She looked round and felt her heart sink. It was the boy from the café. The one who'd been with Kofi. She tried to remember his name, but her mind was blank.

'Hey,' he said.

'Hello,' Charlotte replied.

'All alone?' Ian Mills was smiling. Not a friendly smile. Something predatory about it.

'No. I'm with Danny,' Charlotte said.

'But he's left you all alone,' he went on.

'Don't worry. He'll be back soon.'

'I'd better keep you company,' Mills insisted, still grinning.

Charlotte grimaced. There was something about everything that Ian Mills said that was creepy. Like he was trying to be clever, or to say one thing and mean another.

She cast her eyes over to where Danny had gone with Kofi, willing him to return.

'You and me?' Mills said suddenly. 'A date tonight? Dinner?'

Charlotte shook her head. 'Thanks for asking, but no. I'm busy tonight.'

'Tonight, I said,' Mills went on. But now the smile had gone from his face.

'Thank you. But no.'

Charlotte sensed Mills was about to ask again, but was pausing to think. She was used to older boys asking her out. But she had never felt like it. Or never been asked out by someone she wanted to spend more time with than her friends, Sally, Sophie, Danny, Paul and Kofi.

Mills opened his mouth at last. 'I know the photo fit is Danny,' he said.

Charlotte caught her breath. She looked for

Danny coming across the fields. Then at Mills.

'What?'

'I know that the photo fit in the paper is of Danny. And I know that he was at the house that was burgled earlier. And I know that Paul Wire can identify him.'

Mills took a sheet of paper out of his pocket and unfolded it.

Charlotte said nothing. She had no idea *what* to say. But she knew that if Ian Mills told the police about Danny he could lose everything. So what should she do? Go out with this odious idiot who was a tenth of the person Danny was – or put Danny in danger?

'So?' Mills pushed her.

'What?' Charlotte said.

'One date?' Mills said. 'A meal. Tonight.'

'If I don't?'

'Your friend Danny,' Mills said, pointing to the police car, 'gets a ride in that.'

'And what if I tell Danny what you just told me?'

'You don't. If he knows why you're coming out with me, I tell the police anyway.'

Danny walked with Kofi back to the pitch. There was no sign of the bag. They were pretty sure that it had been stolen. Someone had been in the dressing rooms. They'd vandalized the showers as well as taking who knew what else?

'I must speak to the coach,' Kofi said.

Danny nodded. He wanted to get over to Charlotte and tell her anyway.

He noticed her speaking to someone who was keying something into his phone.

What was this? What was going on?

Then Danny saw the man walking away from Charlotte. Towards him.

He felt even worse when he saw who it was. Ian Mills.

'07700 937 444,' Mills said to Danny.

Danny knew that was Charlotte's number. But he said nothing.

'Charlotte's coming out to dinner with me,' Mills said, laughter in his voice. 'To the Flying Pizza. Do you know it?'

Danny still kept silent.

'Just the two of us,' Mills said. 'Jealous?'

Danny said nothing. But he held Mills' stare until Mills looked away.

'Anyway, got to go,' Mills said, 'I've got a job on tonight. Oh, yes, I hope Kofi finds his bag.'

HOME ALONE

Danny sat in his front room. He was alone.

His sister was out with her new boyfriend.

Holt wasn't answering his phone.

But these things were nothing compared to the fact that Charlotte was out with that idiot Ian Mills. And it was dominating Danny's thoughts.

He just couldn't understand why she would go out with someone like him. It made no sense.

But, after Mills had tried to wind him up, Danny had not said a word about it to Charlotte. And she had not said a word about it to *him*. It wasn't like Danny and Charlotte were going out with each other, but it made Danny feel sick to the stomach, sicker than he had ever felt before. He hated feeling like this. Feelings like this were beyond his control.

Danny even found himself wishing his sister, Emily, was at home to talk to him and take his mind off it. It had to be bad.

But he needed something to clear his head.

Crime.

That was what he needed.

To think about crime.

And the crime on his mind was the burglaries.

Danny walked up to his bedroom. His box of maps and notes were all there. Passing into his bedroom he told himself that, once he was in his room, he was only going to think about solving crimes. Not about Charlotte. Not about what she was doing with Ian Mills.

He could do this.

He settled down, switching on the angle lamp at his desk and turning off the main light. This made him feel like the character from his dad's favourite novel, *The Maltese Falcon* by Dashiel Hammett. The character – Sam Spade – would sit in his office in the light of a small lamp. Drinking whiskey. Thinking. Asking himself questions. Cool as a cucumber.

Danny didn't have whiskey, like Spade would have. But he did have Coke. He popped a can.

Because he had a question to ask *himself*. It was think about this, or go mad.

Why – after Wire had confessed to the burglaries – did Danny not believe Wire was the real culprit?

Surely the case was solved. There was nothing to worry about. Danny had to ask himself what was making him think like that?

Wire had been in the house. That was true. But what, Danny couldn't help but ask, was he doing in the house?

Was he stealing money?

No.

Was he stealing things he could sell to make money?

No.

Why was he so interested in the file? It was just a load of papers to do with City FC. Nothing of value. Except that it was valuable, perhaps, as information.

Maybe that was it. Maybe whoever Wire had been speaking to wanted the papers. Danny cursed himself again for leaving them in the house.

But the usual pattern of burglaries was the theft of money, of valuable objects. Not papers. Not information.

These were different types of burglary. Danny had read about this in the book. There were different types of burglary because they were done by different burglars.

The latest robbery was not like the previous ones. Danny didn't even know if the house they'd been in had anything to do with a footballer. He didn't know who lived there.

So to the next question. Why would Paul Wire claim that he had done all the burglaries?

Danny leaned back and took another swig of Coke.

His mind weaved around all the stories he had ever read, then back to this book he had been reading about why people commit crime.

And that was the question. Why did Wire commit the crimes? Or, why did he say he had?

For glory.

That was why.

Danny was sure of it.

Because he wanted to be known as the thief. Because he liked the notoriety, the fame. And if he couldn't have fame for being a footballer, he would take it for being a criminal.

It seemed crazy to Danny. But there was something in it.

If Danny was to believe it, he needed another suspect. Someone else who would be in a position to steal from footballers and motivated to do it.

Who?

Was it gangsters like they were saying in the chat rooms – the organized criminals who lived for crime, who did it as a job?

Danny wasn't sure. It seemed too easy. And why would they know about footballers and where they lived?

So who else?

Opportunists. People who saw an empty house and decided to rob it.

No, Danny thought. It would be far too much of a coincidence for that to happen to six footballers.

And then something he'd not thought through shuffled back into his head. That it needed to be someone who had access to information about footballers' houses.

Who was that?

One name came to Danny's mind.

Ian Mills.

He had players' addresses, didn't he?

But why would it be him? Danny almost

laughed. He was not much older than Danny. There was no way. Even if he did know all the players' addresses. So what?

No, Danny decided, this was crazy thinking. He was thinking it because he hated Mills. Because Mills was with Charlotte tonight. That was all. How many times had he read a crime book to his dad where a detective missed a vital clue because he hated – or even loved – one of the suspects?

Inspector Morse, for instance. He always fell in love with the woman who turned out to be the murderer in the story, throwing him off the scent.

And yet . . . if it was Mills . . .

Danny stood up.

He was going out.

Now.

Because his head felt hot inside. Because he was losing control of his thoughts. Thoughts that were telling him to go and find Mills. Because, if he was involved, then he was not only a suspect. But a threat.

A threat to Charlotte.

FLYING PIZZA

Danny knew where the Flying Pizza restaurant was. Across the park from where he lived. Two miles. Not far.

Not if you were running.

For the first couple of minutes he struggled with his breathing. It was uneven, gasping. He could feel his calves aching. But once he was off the streets and into the park, he felt better. He'd be able to run it in fifteen minutes. No problem.

But what should he do when he got there?

Interfere?

Just watch?

Do nothing?

Danny decided he could do any of those three things. It was a plan, of sorts. At least he had given himself a few choices.

He speeded up for the second mile. Out of the

green of the park, off the soft grass he'd been running across and on to the tarmac. Harder on the legs. But faster.

Cars raced past him, splashing through the rain that had fallen over the last hour, their headlights picking out puddles as if they were illuminated from below. This was a wealthy part of the city. Not far from the home of the former City FC chairman, Sir Richard Gawthorpe. The cars round here were as posh as the houses.

Two hundred metres from the Flying Pizza, Danny slowed. He'd need to get his breath back, he might want it when he got to the restaurant. He made sure he was on the other side of the road, so he could look in without being so easily seen. There was a gap between a black Range Rover and a white van. Decent cover. He looked into the restaurant through its window, painted to look like vines and grapes growing up the glass.

There were several couples in the restaurant. And some larger groups. Danny studied them closely.

Part of him was pleased not to see Charlotte there. But he knew he was being naive. If Mills and Charlotte were there at least he would know where they were.

He felt anxiety gnawing at his nerves.

Without hesitating he crossed the road and opened the door of the restaurant. He made up a story as he walked. He would pretend to be the son of someone who had not arrived yet.

'Hi,' he said, confident.

'Hello, sir. Are you joining a party here?' A young woman carrying a clipboard smiled at him.

Danny shook his head, then nodded, taking in the smells of food, the heat, the noise. He changed his plan. 'Yes. Mills is the name.' He knew he had to give the surname of the person who had booked the table.

A waiter passed as he mentioned Mills's name. 'They have a-gone,' he said in an Italian accent. Danny wondered if it was real or put on.

'Gone?' he asked.

'Ten minute ago.'

'I'm sorry, sir,' the young woman said.

This was not good. If Mills was dangerous, Danny thought, then what next?

What should he do?

Go to Charlotte's house? Ring her?

He stood looking into the restaurant, seeing food on forks, lips opening, glasses of drink tipped into mouths. But it did nothing for his appetite. He felt sick.

And that was when he realized the young woman and the waiter were still there, looking at him.

Danny blushed. 'Sorry,' he said.

'Not a problem,' the young woman said.

Outside Danny fished out his phone. He dialled Charlotte.

It rang. And rang. And he knew, as he listened, that it was not going to be answered. But he listened to the eight rings Charlotte's phone gave before it went on to the answering service.

'Hi, this is Charlotte. Leave a message or text me.' *Beeeeeeeeep.*

'Text me you're OK,' Danny said. He knew his voice sounded stressed. But he didn't care. 'Please. Just say "Hi" or something.'

Next he texted Kofi. He had to do something. Act. Doing nothing would make him go mad.

> **Do you know where Mills is?**
> **I'm worried about Charlotte.**
> **Danny**

Danny held the phone, staring at it, listening to the sound of traffic rumbling past on the tarmac. He glanced to the left when he saw something move. A bright colour. It was the young woman in the restaurant. She smiled warmly. Danny smiled back, then felt his phone vibrate in his hand.

Hey Danny. Ian's with Charlotte. Leave 'em to it. She needs a man, not a boy.

Danny felt a wave of nausea pass over him.

What was Kofi saying? That Charlotte and Ian should go out? He was sure that Kofi thought Ian was an idiot, like he did.

What was going on?

Danny walked back through the park. He didn't have the energy to run. Didn't have the energy to do much.

His thoughts were all over the place. He felt like he'd lost his best friend. Charlotte going out with Mills. Kofi had gone weird too. It was awful. All too much at once.

And the worst thing was that he could not think. He was normally so clear-headed and thoughtful. He could work things out. But this had thrown him. He felt angry. He felt vulnerable. He felt weak. He felt a lot of things. But he did *not* feel like himself. Not the Danny Harte who would be able to solve this problem.

Because Charlotte was out with Ian Mills, Danny knew he was too emotionally involved. It was beyond him.

As he walked he tried to find a way of working things out for himself.

He went back to his trusted method: how would one of his dad's detective heroes solve it.

Break it down.

Don't try to think about everything at once.

Take each problem on its own.

So what were his problems?

One, Charlotte was with Mills.

Two, he suspected Mills of something.

Three, he was emotionally involved, so was not sure if his suspicion of Mills was biased.

Four, Charlotte was not returning his calls.

Five, Kofi was being weird with him.

And that was where he stopped. He felt a glimmer of something.

Kofi.

Kofi would not be weird with him. Kofi had always been polite and good.

Then it came to him.

Kofi had not texted him.

And why? Because *Mills* had his phone. *Mills* had stolen Kofi's bag earlier at City FC. He had even made a joke about it at the time. Now it made sense. Mills had Kofi's phone: Mills had texted him.

It had to be him.

And because he had done that he could not be trusted. And that meant that, although Danny's feelings were messed up, he could be sure Mills was bad.

What else did he have on Mills?

That he was an idiot.

That he was arrogant.

That he thought all girls loved him.

That he wanted to be famous, even though his football career had failed.

That he was capable of anything, of everything.

That he had Kofi's bag.

The thoughts were coming fast now. Danny felt like he had his mind back. And it was the next thought that made him stop as he walked through the darkening park.

If Mills had Kofi's phone, he would also have his notebook. The one that held Kofi's address.

And what would he do with that?

If, as Danny increasingly suspected, he *was* the real burglar, then he would be planning to visit Kofi's flat. To take all his things. Because he knew that Kofi had new things.

Kofi was the next to be burgled. Mills had said he had a job tonight. He'd been boasting. Taunting Danny. Maybe even letting him know what he was going to do.

That was it.

And if Mills was going to be at Kofi's tonight, perhaps he might be able to shed light on where Charlotte was.

So Danny started walking again, changing direction. Heading for Kofi's flat.

LOCKED IN

The night had been bizarre. That was the best word Charlotte could find for it.

Ian Mills was hideous. Half the time he was boasting about himself, how he was going to be one of the best English players ever and that Forza FC would offer him a contract soon and that he would never play for an English·club again because they didn't have the brains to see how talented he was.

Something like that.

He was full of himself. He even boasted about things that were not the kind of thing you should be proud of.

The rest of the time – when he was not talking about himself – he was asking Charlotte about what films she liked. Or what computer games she was best at. She hated computer games and when she mentioned films she liked he had never heard of them. He seemed only to like extreme violence and horror.

But Charlotte played along. The deal was one date with him and he'd not tell the police about Danny. She didn't trust him to hold out on the deal. But she had no choice.

Eventually after the meal Ian Mills drove Charlotte home. Well, that's what he said he was doing. But instead he took her to a garage, driving in quickly and getting out of the car.

Charlotte went to open the passenger door.

It was locked.

She was a prisoner in his car. In this garage.

Mills was raving, pacing around the garage going on and on about Kofi and how it made him sick that Kofi had a new flat, that Kofi had a new TV, that Kofi must have lots of money lying around the house, that Kofi was out tonight celebrating with Ian's old team-mates, his flat empty.

Suddenly he stormed out, running off and leaving her.

Charlotte knew then that she was not in danger. But that Kofi was.

It was quite clear that Mills was going to his

house. To steal everything he could. Danny had been right. She could see that now.

Charlotte checked her phone. No signal.

She took a small soft bag out of her handbag. Her make-up bag. She took out her nail clippers, pulled the small penknife out of its side, raised it above her head and slashed the soft canvas roof open. It was tough, but, with effort, she got through it.

Then she climbed out of the car and looked at the garage door. Now she had to get through that.

Charlotte studied the garage door. It was the only way out. There was no other door. There were no windows.

She needed to get out. To warn Kofi. To get in touch with Danny.

There was nothing useful in the garage that she could use to get free. The only thing in the garage was the car.

So she used the car.

First, Charlotte released the hand brake. Then she slipped it out of gear.

Then she went round to the front of the car. And pushed.

She had three metres of space to get the car moving. She used all her strength.

The car smashed against the garage door, quickly dislodging it.

It was easy. She'd have to tell Danny about this. He would be impressed.

Next, she eased the garage door open, checking that Mills had gone.

He had.

She was about to leave when she saw that directly down the hill from the garage, there was a large site where a factory and its chimney had been recently demolished. It was a mess. Piles of bricks. Rubble. Iron bars and sheets.

She went to the edge of the site. There was no one there. She made quite sure.

Then she climbed up the slight incline back to the garage, walked round to the front of Mills's car and pushed it again.

It was slow at first. Creeping down the hill. But soon it gathered pace, going faster and faster. Heading for a wall, half knocked down by the demolition.

When the back of the car hit the wall the whole of it was crushed.

Seconds later the wall collapsed. Into the open-topped car. Everything was smashed and filthy.

It was a write-off.

Charlotte smiled. All evening Mills had been talking about his sports car. She had been very bored by that. But she knew it was important to him. She knew that if it was damaged he would feel really bad. But right now she had bigger things to think about. Where had Mills gone? He seemed unhinged, capable of anything.

THE FIGHT

Danny waited outside Kofi's apartments, wondering what to do.

No one was answering the bell he rang at the front of the building.

The apartments were in a building Danny knew well. It had once been a pub. One that families would come to on a Sunday. He remembered his mum and dad bringing him and his sister here when he was a kid. They'd have a meal. And he'd have a Coke. Then they'd walk round the lake to go to the Canal Gardens.

Danny noticed that most of the building was dark. Having circled it, he could see two of the apartments had lights on. So some people were probably home.

But he didn't know which apartment was Kofi's. And there was no way in. So all he could do was wait outside for Kofi. Or, in the worst case, Mills.

It was a cold night. The temperature had dropped much further than it had over previous nights. Danny shivered. There was a breeze coming up from the park, air cooling as it came across the lake.

But this was nothing new to Danny: he had stayed out watching buildings and people in colder weather than this.

There were not many people about. And most of *them* were in cars. Looking for somewhere quiet to spend time in the park. A few others were walking dogs. There were no children.

After half an hour Danny saw Kofi walking, coming down from the main road.

'Kofi!'

Once he had called out, Danny saw his friend smile. He loved that about Kofi. That he was still himself. Even though he'd become a professional footballer. Kofi was the exact opposite to Ian Mills.

Danny spoke quickly. 'I think I know who had your phone. Your bag.'

Kofi looked at him, puzzled. 'How do you know I have lost my phone?'

'I'm guessing it was in your bag.'

Kofi shook his head. 'I have lost my phone, my boots. A lot of things.'

Danny didn't normally like to say someone had done something until he had proven it. But this time it was different. Everything was different about this case. If that was what it was.

'I think it was Ian Mills,' Danny said.

'Ian?'

'Yes.'

'Why would Ian do that? He is my friend.'

'He said some things,' Danny said, 'that made me think it was him. Then I texted your phone. And someone replied back. I am pretty sure it was him.'

'But why would he do it? He has lots of money.' Kofi looked genuinely confused. Clearly he had never doubted Mills for a moment.

Danny shrugged. Should he tell him that he thought Ian Mills hated Kofi because he had everything that Mills had once had, but no longer did?

No. It was just a theory. Something he'd picked up on. But he had no proof.

And maybe he was wrong. Maybe Mills was OK. Maybe Danny just couldn't deal with him taking Charlotte out for a date.

But, even if that was true, should he tell him that he was worried Mills was the real burglar and that he might target Kofi's apartment?

Danny wasn't sure. He felt as if he had no foundation to build on. All the things that were going on had undermined all that.

'Can I come and see your apartment?' Danny asked. At least they could talk. He would enjoy seeing Kofi so nicely set up.

'Yes. You can come in. I am sorry. I should have asked you.'

Danny smiled and they walked towards Kofi's home. Kofi punched a number into a keypad on the door. They walked along the corridor. Everything was new. And clean. The carpet was spotless.

Danny had decided that, once they were inside, he would try to explain honestly to Kofi how he felt about Mills. He would explain that he was not sure if he could judge him properly because of all the things to do with Charlotte.

They reached Kofi's apartment. Kofi took out a single silver key and unlocked the door. 'This is my home.'

THE BURGLAR RETURNS

The burglar swore under his breath when he heard those four words and the two boys entering.

He was already mad – how was it a sixteen-year-old boy from Africa ended up in a luxurious place like this? An old converted house, more like a mansion, bordered by a small lake and a wood. This boy had a swimming pool in his house. The man felt the rage rising inside him now.

It was not fair. All the boy had done in life was kick a ball around in a dusty country, then get a contract at City. But the burglar knew he had to get control of himself. He knew he had to be calm.

He'd already let himself go, slashed the plasma screen, snapping off all the breakable things he could on the stereo system, even pouring bleach on Kofi's clothes.

He had not done this before. Not broken things on purpose.

He would usually just go in, find valuable things and take them.

But this was different.

This was personal.

And now Kofi was here. Him and that pathetic friend of his.

Now was his chance to get even.

DILEMMA

Danny followed Kofi inside.

As he turned to take off his shoes, ultra-conscious that they would be dirty and this was a very clean place, he noticed something move above Kofi's head. And then he saw Kofi go down hard on the floor. And standing directly behind Kofi, a baseball bat in his right hand, he saw Ian Mills.

But there was no time to think about that. Or about helping Kofi. Because Mills was on to him, taking advantage of Danny's surprise. He leapt over Kofi, who lay on the floor, unconscious or dead, and struck at Danny with the bat.

Danny leapt back, but Mills still caught him. On the shoulder. A hard blow that sent pain shooting down Danny's arms and legs.

Danny fell back against the wall. Mills moved forward, lashing at him.

Danny dodged again. This time successfully. Mills hit the wall hard, punching such a deep hole into the plasterwork that he had to pull hard to release his baseball bat.

And that gave Danny time. Time to move back and think of a way out of this.

He couldn't leave: he needed to help Kofi.

But he had no weapon.

What could he use? Where would one be?

The kitchen.

Danny turned to push open a door. He hoped it was the kitchen. And it was.

He ran in and grabbed a knife from the counter top. It felt strange in his hand. Like he should not be doing this.

But what choice did he have?

Danny waited in the kitchen. He knew Mills would be in any moment.

He was right.

Mills stood in the doorway and eyed Danny's knife.

'What are you going to do with that?' he asked.

Danny said nothing. Because he had no idea really.

'She was good fun,' Mills said next.

Danny looked at Mills in disgust. Then he saw him step forward, his baseball bat raised. Danny had to choose. Try to defend himself with the knife. Or take a beating.

There was no debate.

Danny dropped the knife on the floor and kicked it behind him.

Mills came at Danny fast, the baseball bat in his hand hurtling through the air.

But Danny chose not to run away. He had no knife. But he'd had no intention of ever using a knife. He knew he could outwit Mills. He just needed a bit of luck.

So Danny ran at Mills. Towards the swinging bat.

A split second later he heard it hit the kitchen counter behind him, splitting wood and metal.

He had got underneath Mills and the bat missed him altogether. And he was close enough that he could make the next move.

He felt Mills's body over his. Mills had used

all his strength to attack Danny. Now he was off balance. And Danny had the advantage.

Danny used all his rage – rage at Mills for all he had done and everything he was saying – to lift the former youth footballer off his feet and to slam him into the wall.

And he slammed him hard. As hard as he could. He wanted to put him down now. Leave him with no second chances.

He felt the shock waves of Mills's impact with the wall go through him too. He heard Mills moan. Then he heard him hit the floor.

Danny stepped back. He was winded and almost overcome by the adrenalin that was running freely in his blood now.

Mills was still conscious, but his breathing was deep and heavy. It was a good thing that there was no way he was getting up. Because Danny had little left.

But Mills could still speak. 'This isn't over,' he moaned.

'No?' Danny asked, reaching for the phone that was on the wall to his left.

'Phoning your girlfriend?' Mills went on.

Danny shook his head, replacing the handset. 'She's my friend, not my girlfriend.'

'No, that's right,' Mills said. 'Maybe she's my girlfriend.'

'I doubt it.' Danny was confident now. He knew Charlotte would never have anything to do with a person like Mills. He must have coerced her into going on the date. He had no doubts.

Mills eased himself up, so he was sitting with his back to the wall.

'We had a good time tonight,' he said.

'I doubt that too,' Danny said, resisting the base impulse to kick Mills now he was down.

'Don't you want to know where she is?'

Danny picked up the handset again. 'I'm calling an ambulance for Kofi. And the police.'

'The police? What for?'

'For you. Breaking and entering. Assault. Attempted GBH.'

'You've been watching too many police shows on the TV,' Mills scoffed.

Danny didn't respond to Mills. He dialled 9 twice, his finger poised to hit it a third time.

'You really don't want to do that.' Mills sounded different now. There was a dark menace in his voice. He was about to make a threat: Danny could predict it. 'You do that and I tell them who the photo fit is of. *And* I show them the pictures I have of you on my phone. Hanging around footballers' houses. And what with your police record . . . well, you've had it. Haven't you?'

Danny kept his finger over the 9.

But he knew he had some thinking to do before he pressed it. Mills had found his Achilles' heel.

'In fact, I think I'll claim you were my right-hand man,' Mills said.

Danny could feel the anger rising in him. That rage again. Like a force of blood rushing upwards. Like a volcano.

But he knew he had to calm himself. Mills was a wind-up merchant. He'll have done this on the football pitch. Wound players up. Got them to lose their cool. And why? So that whoever he was winding up made bad decisions, made things worse.

So what should he do?

He had to make a decision. A *good* decision.

He could let Mills go so that he didn't drag Danny into the police investigation – and leave Danny losing more than Mills would. Because Danny might lose his freedom too. He could lose his as yet clean police record. Worst of all, he would lose the chance to be a police officer in the future.

And that, for Danny, was everything.

He couldn't really call the police, could he? He had too much to lose.

He needed help. So he turned to what had worked before.

He tried to think of the numerous crime books he'd read. Where fictional detectives were caught in dilemmas like this. What had they done?

Done the right thing?

Or saved themselves?

And each one that came to mind had not done the right thing. They had all saved themselves, arguing that this would be better in the long run. That they would be able to solve more crimes if they did save themselves.

But Danny could think of no detective he wanted to emulate in this. It was pointless. Because the voice of his dad was in his head now. And the voice was saying, *Do the right thing*.

Danny pressed 9.

He needed no more thought.

'Ambulance, please. And police,' he said, looking into Mills's eyes again, until Mills looked away.

UNDER ARREST

Keeping an eye on Mills, convinced he was going nowhere, Danny went to check up on Kofi.

His friend was sitting up, his back to the wall.

'Good,' Danny said. 'You're OK?'

When Kofi put his arms to his side to get up, Danny rested his hand on his friend's shoulder.

'Stay there. There's an ambulance coming. Let them check you out first.'

Kofi nodded. 'What about Ian?'

'He'll be OK. A few broken ribs, I expect. That's why he can't move much. But the police will be here soon.'

'It was good you were here,' Kofi said.

'I know.'

Then they heard the sirens. Coming their way.

Danny was surprised how focused the police were.

Once they had checked out that Danny and Kofi were OK, they moved on to Mills. Mills had been lifted on to a wheelchair by the paramedics. He was OK. Danny watched him carefully. He was wondering what Mills would say to incriminate him.

'Are you Ian Mills?' one of the officers asked. He was short and lean. He had the physique of a long-distance runner.

'I am,' Mills said.

'I am arresting you for the abduction and false imprisonment of Charlotte Duncan –'

'The what?' Danny shouted, making the police officers jump.

'I've got her,' Mills said, smiling at Danny. 'You can arrest me for that. And you can arrest me for all the burglaries of the footballers. Paul Wire had nothing to do with any of them. There's no way he's getting the credit for them.'

Danny lunged at Mills, grabbing him by his clothes. 'Where is she? If you've hurt her, I'll kill you.'

His head had definitely gone this time. It had been hard enough thinking that Charlotte wanted to spend time with someone like him. But the idea that he had harmed her was too much.

'I'm here.'

The voice came from behind Danny.

Danny let go of Mills, pushing him away. Then he turned round.

Charlotte was standing in the doorway. With Kofi. And unharmed.

After over an hour answering police questions, the police offered to take Danny and Charlotte home in one of their cars. But Danny said he wanted to walk.

He asked Charlotte if she would come too.

Someone from City FC had arrived to see if Kofi was all right. And now that the media were there in force, Danny wanted to get away. He checked for Holt as they walked through the park, but he was not among the growing phalanx of reporters.

Danny wondered why he wasn't.

As they walked, Charlotte put her arm in Danny's. She hadn't done that before. But it felt OK.

Once Charlotte had explained what had happened to her – and Danny had stopped laughing at the pictures she had taken of Mills's car – she started to ask Danny questions.

'So if Mills said he was going to get you into trouble for being involved in the burglaries, why didn't he?'

Danny frowned. 'I think he wanted all the glory for himself.'

'Glory? He'll end up in prison.'

'He will. But I think he's happier in prison and famous for something, than out of prison and not famous.'

'I don't get that,' Charlotte said.

'Nor me,' Danny agreed, 'but that's how he works.'

Danny thought back to Wire. He and Mills were remarkably similar in their strange need for notoriety. What had Wire been doing claiming responsibility for the burglaries if it was Mills who had been doing it all along – in fact what was he actually doing in the house in the first place? Danny couldn't put the City FC papers Wire had been so desperate for out of his mind. There was a lead there. He knew it. But one run-in with the police this week was enough for Danny. He would leave it for now.

Eventually they reached Danny's house. There was a familiar car at the front.

'Holt's here,' Danny said. 'He must have come straight here to talk to me.'

Charlotte said nothing in reply as they went up the garden path. The front-room curtains were drawn.

Danny opened the front door.

His sister shot out of the living room, looking guilty.

'Is Anton here?' Danny asked.

'Er . . . yeah,' Emily said. 'I thought you were Mum and Dad.'

'They're not back for two days,' Danny said. What was going on?

Charlotte followed Danny into the front room.

Anton was sitting there, a cup of tea in front of him. He smiled at Danny. It was a funny smile and Danny was not quite sure what it meant.

'So you heard?' Danny said.

'Er . . . about what?' Holt said.

'Mills. The attack on Kofi. Charlotte,' Danny gasped.

Holt stood up, looking over Danny's shoulder. 'Charlotte. What? Are you OK?'

Charlotte smiled at Holt, then at Danny. 'I'm fine,' she said.

Now Holt was firing questions. What had

happened to Kofi? How was Charlotte involved? What had the police said? Was someone from the *Evening Post* there?

Once Holt had finished Danny decided *he* wanted to ask a question. 'So, if you didn't know any of that was going on, why did you come round to see me?'

Danny heard Charlotte laugh, then Emily. He looked at Holt, who had managed to keep a straight face.

Danny looked at Charlotte. 'What?'

Charlotte glanced at Holt, then at Emily. Then she raised her eyebrows at Danny.

It was a message. How had he missed it? Emily was going out with Anton!

And Danny could feel himself blushing. Heavily.

'Great detective *you* are,' Charlotte said, linking her arm into his again.

THANK-YOUS

I would like to thank several people for helping me with this book. My wife, Rebecca; the writers' group Sophie Hannah, James Nash and Rachel Connor; three of my readers who commented on the early chapters, Amber Bytheway, Jack Prangley and Alice Bamber.

I also need to thank Ghyllgrove Junior School in Basildon. Their Football Writers – led by their amazing teacher, Mrs Diane Baker – read the whole thing together and gave me some great ideas, as well as helping me decide to drop something major that didn't work. That is why the book is dedicated to them.

Thank you also to David and Rebecca at Luxton Harris – for everything they do.

And thank you to Kester Aspden, award-winning author, who gave me lots of ideas for this book, as well as pointing me in the direction of some great criminology books that Danny might enjoy, in particular *Breaking and Entering: Burglars on Burglary* by Paul Cromwell and James Olson.

Ten REAL football crimes

1. In the mid-1990s several English Premiership evening games had to be postponed mid-game because betting syndicates tampered with the floodlights, switching the lights off.

2. In 1966 the World Cup trophy was stolen from a window in Birmingham, where it was being displayed to promote the World Cup finals. It was found later by a dog.

3. Several Liverpool players have been burgled in the last few years while they played away in Europe. Most notably, Steven Gerrard's wife was confronted by four masked men in 2007.

4. Former Everton and West Ham star Mark Ward was jailed for renting a house that was used to store £1 million's worth of illegal drugs.

5. In 2007 a friend of German football supremo Franz Beckenbauer was shot dead in South Africa as the country prepared for the World Cup preliminary draw. On the same day the German team manager had his briefcase stolen.

6. In 2007 Newcastle midfielder Joey Barton was jailed for 74 days for having a fight outside a Liverpool nightclub.

7. In 1994 the Columbian defender Andres Escobar was shot dead, following his scoring of a notorious own goal in the 1994 World Cup finals. Many think it was because drug barons lost a lot of money because of the goal.

8. In 2008 another Colombian player shot dead a fan who'd heckled him about how badly he had been playing. He was jailed.

9. In 1970 Bobby Moore, the England captain, was arrested in Colombia and charged with stealing jewellery. He was quickly released, once it became clear he had been set up.

10. In 2007 the former Manchester City keeper Ashley Timms admitted to trying to blackmail a Premier League footballer, claiming he had an interesting video of him.

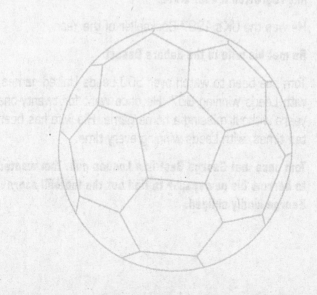

Ten things you (possibly) didn't know about TOM PALMER

Tom was possibly left as newborn in a box at the door of an adoption home in 1967.

He has got an adopted dad and a step-dad, but has never met his real dad.

Tom's best job – before being an author – was a milkman. He delivered milk for nine years.

He once scored two goals direct from the corner flag in the same game. It was very windy.

Tom did not read a book by himself until he was seventeen.

In 1990 Tom wrecked his knee while playing for Bulmershe College in Reading. He didn't warm up and has regretted it ever since.

He was the UK's 1997 Bookseller of the Year.

He met his wife in the Sahara Desert.

Tom has been to watch over 500 Leeds United games, with Leeds winning 307. He once went for twenty-one years without missing a home game. His wife has been ten times, with Leeds winning every time.

Tom once met George Best in a London pub. Tom wanted to borrow his newspaper to find out the football scores. George kindly obliged.